# WAGON MOUND:
# DO OR DIE

## THE COWAN FAMILY SAGA – BOOK 2

Russell J. Atwater

# Contents

# Chapter One
# No Survivors

"Trent, I always know where to find you," Pat called out as he rode up to the Cowans' wagon.

Becky sat on the wagon seat, while her mother and father walked on either side of the oxen. Trent rode Tex alongside the wagon, while Lobo, his dog, chased mice that the wagon and oxen scared up from the grass. Trent paused his conversation with the golden-haired daughter of Bruce Cowan, the wagon train master, to give his brother an annoyed look.

The past month on the Santa Fe Trail had seen Becky's father, Bruce, transformed from a greenhorn bricklayer from Boston into a seasoned wagon master. No longer did he shy away from danger or tough decisions. Bruce no longer relied on his double-barrel shotgun. He now wore a Colt Army and could shoot center when called upon to draw his iron.

"I have to consult with Bruce often, Pat, as you should know," Trent said and showed a bit of irritation with his younger brother. "The Cimarron Cutoff is coming up soon. Bruce has to decide whether to take it or proceed up into the mountains."

"Hmm, I guess Becky is giving you a second opinion," Pat said.

"Yeah, well, taking the cutoff will be hard on the womenfolk," Trent said.

"Trent, I'm not a delicate flower like I was back in Boston. I can take the hardships of the trail as well as any of the other women in the wagon train."

"It sounds like Bruce has already decided to take the cutoff," Pat said.

"I have!" Bruce called out from beside the second team of oxen. He walked beside a huge Red Durham ox. "We are taking the cutoff. It saves ten days of travel. Is there a reason you rode all the way from the back of the train, Pat?"

"Yeah, Bruce, the miller lost a wheel. We have to stop until he gets it fixed." *Just what happens – times 50*

"Dang it! Another day, another delay. That's one of the reasons I'm taking the cutoff. To make up for the time we lose with repairs," Bruce said.

"Do you hear that?" Pat suddenly called out.

"Rifle shots!" Trent shouted.

Bruce shook his head. "Goodness, what now? This can't be good. Lois, Becky, get in the back of the wagon. Trent, you and Pat ride out and see what's happening." *look who is giving orders.*

"Pa," Wes said as he rode up on Major, his Quarter Horse. "Is that smoke on the horizon?"

Trent answered, "Yup, it's smoke all right."

"Be careful. Shoot first," Bruce shouted as Trent and Pat spurred their mounts into a gallop. *wow – what a change!*

Trent thought he would never hear old Bruce say shoot first. But the bricklayer from Boston's attitude had changed *me either* in the past month. The dangers and rigors of the trail had hardened Bruce in both body and soul.

Pat took the lead. His spotted bangtail stallion could sprint like the wind. Tex, Trent's Appaloosa had longer legs and could run all day. As they approached a knoll, a rider topped the summit, galloping toward them. A moment later, the two brothers saw why he burned leather: ten Comanches, whooping and waving rifles, charged into view.

Riding at a dead gallop, Trent lifted his Sharps to his shoulder and fired. Before the deafening roar of the .50 caliber buffalo rifle died, the lead Comanche pitched backward off his spotted pony. The rest of the men with him reacted immediately. They jerked their ponies to a ground-plowing halt.

Trent and Pat pulled up as the rider barreled toward them. Twenty feet from them, the rider pitched sideways off his buckskin gelding. He hit the ground hard and didn't rise. Trent and Pat stopped their mounts a few yards away from the fallen man. Trent stayed on his horse with the Sharps lifted to his shoulder as Pat dismounted and rushed to the man lying unmoving in the grass.

"I must have hit their chief," Trent called out to Pat as his brother bent over the man. "The Comanches are loading him on his pony. I think they have lost the will to fight. How's the settler?" Trent asked upon seeing the man's clothes.

"He's bleeding from at least three bullet wounds!" Pat said. He lifted the man's head. "What happened, pardner?" Can't you tell?

Trent could see the man's lips move as he tried to talk. However, blood ran out of his mouth and down his chin.

"He's dead," Pat said a moment later as he lowered the man's head.

"The Comanches have cleared out. Let's ride over and see what's burning before they decide to have a go at us again," Trent said.

"Nah, they will have to elect another chief before they fight again. It's the Comanche way. Not much will deter an attack except the death of their war chief," Pat said.

"To tell the awful truth, I didn't know he was the war chief. I guess today is our lucky day, Pat."

"Yup, if we keep having such fine luck, we'll have to take up poker," Pat said as he vaulted onto his mustang. "Let's ride over the knoll and see what's afire."

"Wagons for sure," Trent said as he spurred Tex into a gallop.

"You're as right as rain," Pat said as they topped the incline.

Below them lay ten burning wagons. Even from afar, Trent spotted women and children lying motionless among the bodies of their husbands and fathers. "The Comanche are worse than the Apaches, Pat."

"Yeah, I read where the Apaches used to live hereabouts, but the Comanches and Kiowa drove them into southern Texas," Pat said as he slowed his horse to a walk to keep from trampling on the bodies sprawled like rag dolls around the burning wagons while he checked the bodies.

"No need to do that. Lobo is searching for anyone alive," Trent said and nodded at the big wolf-dog as he moved from body to body, sniffing. "I'd rather face five Apaches than one Comanche," Trent said as he stared down at the settlers while Lobo tried to find life in one of them. Trent added, "We shouldn't let the women in the wagon train see this."

Pat shook his head. "Yup, your gal Becky might not be so sure of herself if she witnessed the results of this massacre."

Trent pointed the barrel of his rifle to the right. "We ain't out of the woods, yet, Pat."

Pat glanced to the right. "Hmm, I count at least twenty Comanches."

"Should I put one in the dirt?" Trent asked. Although Trent usually took the lead in matters concerning Indians, he deferred to his young brother. Pat looked like their full-blooded Yaqui mother, while Trent looked like their Scottish father. Upon meeting them, no one would ever suspect they were brothers.

Pat shook his head. "No, they're milling around like a wolf pack that just lost its alpha. If you put another one in the dirt, it might make them angry enough to attack without a war chief. Best we let them be for the moment."

Hearing horses, both Trent and Pat looked back down the trail in time to see Bruce, Wes, and Ralf ride over the summit.

"The cavalry," Trent said.

"The Comanches are leaving," Pat said.

"Yup, they probably think Ralf is a grizzly bear on a horse and decided to hightail it back to their tipis instead of tangling with him," Trent said."

Pat nodded. "Yeah, I feel sorry for his horse."

"Dadburn it! What an awful sight!" Bruce swore and turned his gaze away from the bodies. "Of course, we have to bury these families before the wagons pass this way," he added. "Wes, ride back and tell them to circle. Once they're in position, send the men here with shovels to bury the fallen settlers."

"Yes, Pa."

Trent nodded to the right. A lone mounted Comanche watched them. "He's smart. He's out of range, even for the Sharps. I guess he's encountered buffalo hunters before."

Bruce shook his head. "Will they attack our wagon train?"

"Not unless there are more than what Pat and I saw. Of course, they may be riding for reinforcements. I sort of doubt they're going to let me killing their war chief slide. Comanches are big on revenge."

"And patience," Pat added.

"Yup, they'll come at us when we least expect it," Trent agreed.

"Then, boys, I guess we have to be prepared," Bruce said. "While we're waiting for men and shovels, let's see what, if anything, can be salvaged from the wagons.

As Trent dismounted, Lobo walked up and lowered his head to be patted. "Yeah, it's sad," Trent said as he stroked the big dog's head before joining the other men attempting to salvage tools from the charred wagons.

By the time they finished burying the dead, the sun hung like a blazing fireball in the west, just past the midway point. Trent had a blister on his left hand from using a shovel. Pat had opted to scout in the direction the lone Comanche had finally departed. Trent wasn't surprised his brother found another task. Pat looked down upon work like digging holes in the ground. And like their Yaqui mother, he thought one should bury the dead above the ground.

"I hope Lois has plenty of vittles cooked up for lunch," Bruce said. "I'm hungry enough to eat a shoe."

"Yeah, well, sometimes, I can't tell what my wife cooks from a shoe sole," Ralf said as he shouldered his shovel and walked with Bruce and Trent back to their horses.

"Hmm," Trent said. "From what I see, your wife's cooking hasn't stunted you."

"You know, I still owe you a licking..." Ralf reminded Trent.

"I see Pat," Wes said as he joined them at their horses. "And from the speed he's riding, I don't think it's good news he's bringing us."

Bruce shook his head. "Yeah, I bet he found a slew of Comanches."

Pat's face, as usual, didn't reveal anything as he dismounted.

"Well, are you going to tell us what you found, or do I have to pull it out of you?" Bruce asked.

"A group of about one hundred Comanches are having a powwow to pick a new war chief about five miles to the north," Pat said as he glanced from Trent to Bruce.

"Will they attack?" Bruce asked.

"Probably," Pat said. "More than likely tonight."

Bruce shook his head as he glanced over at Trent. "We won't survive a night attack, will we?"

"Nope," Trent said and then turned to Pat. "I guess we'll have to make them attack before nightfall."

"Sharps?" Pat asked.

Trent nodded. "Yup and a fast retreat."

Bruce shook his head. "Don't tell me you're going to force them to attack?"

"We can't wait for a night assault."

"Dang it. Some of us are going to get killed," Bruce said.

"But not all of us," Pat said.

"Pat's right. If they swarm us at night, then it would be a massacre. The Comanches would kill everyone and burn the wagons, just like they did to this wagon train," Trent said. "Bruce, you need to get back and prepare the men and women to defend the wagons. Pat and I will head out and stir them up."

"The women?" Bruce asked.

"Yeah, and anyone old enough to shoot a rifle or pistol," Pat answered.

"I'm going with you," Wes said.

Trent shook his head. "No, you help your pa get the men ready. Anyway, if Pat and I don't make it back, they're going to need you blazing away with that Peacemaker."

Wes nodded as he watched Trent and Pat mount their horses. "If you get scalped, Becky is going to be unhappy," he told Trent.

"Not as unhappy as I'll be," Trent replied. He glanced down at Lobo. "Come on, let's get some exercise," he added before he urged Tex into a gallop.

Later, when they topped a small hill, the brothers spotted the Comanches camped by a shallow stream north of the Santa Fe Trail. Ponderosa pines lined the bank of the stream, providing shade from the relentless sun. The men were bunched together in the shade.

"It's a distance," Pat said. "I'm going to have to dismount to make a shot."

"I'll get off Tex too. I can reload faster," Trent said. When Trent dismounted, Lobo took the opportunity to lick him in the face.

"I bet Lobo kisses you more often than Becky," Pat said and snickered.

"You best hush, brother," Trent said good-naturedly as he lay in the grass and rested the barrel of his Sharps on a rock. "This will do fine. You see those two Comanches with the long feather headdresses standing as though they are addressing the rest?"

"Yup, I see them," Pat said.

"Let's put holes in them first. After that, we'll fire at will," Trent said.

"I'll take the one on the right. You go first," Pat said.

A moment of silence followed as Trent took careful aim. A moment after he squeezed the trigger, Pat fired his buffalo rifle. Like dominoes, one of the standing Comanches fell, and then the other one hit the dirt.

The men all sprung to their feet as the sound of the Sharps echoed across the prairie. Two more Comanches got knocked off their feet when the big-bore bullets smashed into them. Suddenly, the men sprinted for their horses like swarming ants.

"Time to hightail it back to the wagons," Trent shouted as he stood.

Suddenly, a Comanche sprung up from the grass, waving a tomahawk as he charged Trent. However, a gray streak intercepted the charging man, knocking him to the ground.

Before the Comanche could use his tomahawk on Lobo, the wolf-dog ripped his throat out.

"Come on," Pat shouted as he stuffed his rifle into his scabbard and drew his right pistol. He covered Trent as his brother mounted Tex.

"Leave him, Lobo," Trent shouted as he spurred Tex into a full gallop with Pat hot on his heels.

# Chapter Two
# Shooting Center

Trent turned in the saddle, lifted his Sharps, and fired.

The Comanche who had been gaining on them slumped forward and slipped off his pony. Immediately, Trent reloaded, aimed, and fired the buffalo rifle again. The bullet knocked another warrior backward off his pony. The death of two of their members threw the rest of the charging Comanches into a yelling frenzy.

"They ain't going to stop now," Trent mumbled as Tex neared the wagons.

"Over here!" Bruce shouted as he waved Trent and Pat toward an opening between his two wagons. The moment Trent, Pat, and Lobo sprinted through the opening, Bruce and Wes rolled barrels of flour to block the opening and give cover.

Trent leaped off Tex and ran to where Bruce and Wes stood, both with a Winchester ready to fire.

"Dang it. There must be a hundred of them," Bruce said.

Instead of answering, both Trent and Pat raised their Sharps and fired.

"Two more down," Wes said as he waited for the Comanches to come within range of the smaller-caliber Winchesters.

"Bruce, call everyone to this side of the wagon. We need to kill as many as we can during their first charge," Trent said before he fired again.

At Bruce's call, men and women rushed across the center area and took up positions just as the Comanches came into rifle range.

The blast of over sixty rifles echoed like thunder across the prairie as the Comanches charged straight at the wagons, firing their rifles and yelling. Men and horses caught bullets in the sudden killing field. Twenty-five Comanches lay dead or wounded when the smoke cleared. Riderless horses wandered among the carnage.

The wall of bullets stunned the Comanches. They turned back and rode out of the range of the Sharps and milled around.

"Tell everyone to get back to their wagons," Trent shouted at Bruce. "They ain't going to charge in one group again."

After Bruce gave the orders to the settlers, he walked back over to Trent. "Where did you learn military tactics?"

"My father was an officer in the Scots Guard," Trent said as he reached down to pat Lobo, who stood next to him.

"Well, you sure gave them a surprise. Look at them. They don't know what to do," Bruce said as he stared at the milling group of Comanches.

"They will want a truce so they can collect their dead and wounded," Pat said.

"Will they attack again?" Bruce asked.

"It depends on the war chief. If he doesn't want to lose any more men, he might call off the attack."

"I've got an idea," Trent said.

"Let's hear it," Bruce said as he watched the milling Comanches.

"I'll have Pat offer them the Sharps we took from Jack Blake's wagon," Trent explained. "He can demonstrate its range and show the war chief how to reload. We can also give him several boxes of shells."

Bruce shook his head. "I don't know. Putting a long-range rifle in the hands of the Comanches sounds risky. They're sure to use it against the cavalry."

"That's true, but I haven't seen many who could hit center. They grew up using bows and lances. Switching to a pistol or rifle doesn't come easy," Pat said.

"Is one rifle going to be enough?" Bruce asked.

"It might be if you throw in a case of the whiskey you're carrying in your second wagon for trading purposes," Trent said.

Bruce nodded. "Sure, if it will save lives. We lost Don Burns during the charge. He took a bullet in the chest. His wife is ill. She's going to need help with the oxen. If the Comanche mount another attack, we could lose a dozen men or even more," Bruce said. "Wes, go fetch a case of whiskey," Bruce added.

"Maybe they won't call for a truce," Ralf called out from his seat on a barrel of flour.

Pat pointed toward the Comanches. "A rider is coming. It's the war chief. He's got a peace lance."

Trent smiled. "Never doubt my brother's knowledge," he said.

Bruce shook his head but didn't say anything.

"Here's the case of whiskey, Pa!" Wes said as he hurried back from the wagon. He glanced at Pat. "I'll go with you to meet the war chief and carry the whiskey."

Pat glanced at Bruce. *Dumb Kid & Dumb Dad*

Bruce shrugged. "It's okay with me. If they try something, Wes can give you a hand."

Pat nodded to Wes. "Come on. We'll walk out to meet him."

"The Bruce of a month ago would never have let Wes go out to meet a war chief with Pat," Trent said as they watched the two walk away from the wagons.

"A month ago, Wes was a boy. He's a man now," Bruce admitted. *He's 15 – hardly a man – even in the west*

"Where is Wes going?" Lois called from behind the wagon seat.

"He's out with Pat. Now don't worry, Trent is going to cover them with his rifle. Get back and hunker down with Becky in case they mount another attack."

"Don't you want me and Becky to help reload for you?" Lois asked. *Who's the Boss – Trent or Bruce?*

Bruce glanced at Trent.

"That's what the other women are doing," Trent said then lowered his voice. "I don't particularly like it, but if we get overrun, they won't survive. Better to catch a bullet than die at the hands of the Comanches," Trent added.

Bruce shook his head. "You paint a pretty grim picture, Trent."

Trent shrugged. "It's the truth."

Bruce glanced at the wagon. "Yeah, that's a good idea. Get Becky and sit behind the barrels of flour. You should be safe there to reload if they mount another attack. Which, I pray, they won't."

As Becky and Lois settled down behind the barrels, Trent turned his attention back to Pat and Wes. They had met the war chief. Pat was using sign language to communicate with him. From a distance, Trent could catch only a sign now and then. He thought the conversation might be going well.

Trent knew Pat was making progress when his brother handed the Comanche the Sharps. The chief examined the rifle carefully before finally handing it back to Pat. Trent watched as Pat showed the chief how to load the rifle before he handed it back up to the mounted man.

The war chief aimed at a scrawny Ponderosa pine at least 300 yards from their position and, after a long pause, fired. The bullet snapped off the pine about three feet from the ground.

Trent turned to Bruce. "I think that will seal the deal!"

"Dang it, I hope so!" Bruce exclaimed.

As Trent and the settlers watched, the conversation went on for several more minutes, until finally the war chief motioned for one of his warriors to come and fetch the case of whiskey. Pat and Wes waited until the war chief turned his pony around and headed back to his men before he and Wes turned back to the wagons. As Pat and Wes approached the wagon, a cheer went up from the settlers.

Pat shook his head as he approached Trent.

"What's the matter?"

"If Chief Long Knife had missed that pine sapling, he would have ordered an attack."

"You did a great job," Bruce said as he hurried forward to shake Pat's hand. "You saved our bacon for sure."

"He didn't give us safe passage through his territory, did he?" Trent asked.

"No, he said we had killed a lot of his men, and some of their brethren would want revenge. What he did promise was that he would keep them from staging a mass attack," Pat said.

"That's not good," Trent said. "Comanches are masters of the ambush. Men who lost a brother, uncle, or father might attack the wagon train knowing they will die. They will see it as an honorable death."

"Bruce," Pat said. "You should instruct all the settlers who are outside of the wagons to go armed at all times, even the women. If they don't know how to shoot a pistol, their husbands should immediately show them. People are going to die before we get out of this tribe's territory, I can assure you."

Bruce shook his head as he watched Comanches returning to the killing field to collect the bodies of their dead companions. One stood on the back of his horse and made a show of cutting off his hair and tossing it on the ground.

"That one will surely seek revenge. He's preparing himself to die and go to the happy hunting ground," Pat said.

"Why did he cut off his hair?" Becky asked as she stood up from behind the flour barrels.

"To show that the decision of Chief Long Knife dishonors him," Pat explained. As he explained, several more warriors joined the dissenter and cut off their hair.

"Dadburn it! At least twelve more are cutting off their hair," Bruce said. "We need to get out of their territory as soon as possible. If they're not going to attack us right away, we should get the wagons rolling again."

"Yup," Trent agreed. "Come on, Pat, let's pass the word."

"Do you mind if I walk with you, Trent?" Becky asked.

Trent smiled. "Sure, come along. You probably need to exercise your legs after being cramped up inside the wagon."

Wes glanced over at Pat and rolled his eyes as the two walked away. *I did too!*

"Becky has got Trent roped," Pat said without changing his stoic facial expression.

"Roped but not hogtied. He can still get away," Wes said and chuckled as they walked in the opposite direction to spread the warning among the settlers.

"Do you really think some of those men who cut their hair will attack the wagons?" Wes asked.

"They will," Pat said. "It's going to get bloody, Wes. Facing one Comanche willing to die is worse than facing five fired up normal men. You're going to have to have eyes in the back of your head the next couple of days."

# Chapter Three
# Revenge

Finished making their rounds, Trent and Pat walked up to the cookfire. The Cowan family paused in the middle of a meal of biscuits and bacon gravy to make room for the brothers.

"Here," Becky said as she dipped gravy over four biscuits and handed the metal plate to Trent while Lois served Pat.

"Thanks, I'm hungry enough to eat a bear," Trent said as he took the plate. He moved over to sit beside Bruce. "We'll be at Fort Dodge tomorrow. Do you still plan on taking the Cimarron Cutoff?"

"Yep, it cuts ten days off the trip. Some settlers are already getting low on supplies and don't have money to restock at Fort Dodge tomorrow. It'll help them."

"Maybe those who are running out of supplies should peel off tomorrow and stay in Fort Dodge. There's land to settle near the fort," Trent said. *With Comanches!*

"I'll ask them, but I think, like me, they have their hearts set on farther west. Maybe not to California, but at least to Texas or the New Mexico Territory."

"Well, just remind everyone that between the Cimarron River and the Canadian River, there's little to no water. If the wagons don't have extra barrels for hauling water, they shouldn't continue. And even with extra water, we might lose some oxen if we run into a sandstorm."

Bruce looked puzzled. "Why is a sandstorm dangerous for the oxen?" *Oh did he just ask That!*

"The dust! If it clogs an ox's nose, he'll overheat and die. Their bodies are cooled down different from horses and mules. Dust don't matter much to them, but it has killed many oxen," Trent explained as he offered his leftovers to Lobo, who had walked over and sat beside him.

"Your dog looks healthy. I never see you feed him much," Bruce said.

Trent nodded. "Yup, he runs down jackrabbits and prairie dogs. He can pretty much take care of himself." After Lobo finished scarfing down the scraps, Trent walked over and handed his plate to Lois. "It was delicious, Miss Lois."

Lois shook her head. "Becky cooked supper while I helped Bruce take care of the oxen."

Trent glanced over at Becky. "Hmm, ride a horse and cook, not bad for a girl from Boston."

Becky picked up one of the remaining biscuits and threw it at Trent. Lobo leaped up and caught it in midair. Everyone laughed as Lobo gulped down the biscuit.

Bruce stood up. "Okay, daylight comes fast. Let's all get some shut-eye." He stood up and walked over to Lois and reached down. She took his hand. "Come on, dear, let's get some sleep."

"Wes," Pat called out. "Let's go and make the rounds before we hit the blankets."

Wes winked at Pat. "Trent, are you coming?"

"Go ahead. I'll go the opposite direction and meet up with you."

"Yup, I thought that would be your answer," Wes said teasingly.

"My brother's still a brat," Becky said.

Trent chuckled. "He'll be one to ride the river with when he's got a few more years under his belt."

Becky smiled and started to reply. Instead, she screamed as she pointed toward the prairie.

Trent shifted his rifle from the crook of his arm as he turned into the face of a dozen charging Comanches. He fired. The bullet from his rifle knocked one of the men off his feet. Lacking time to reload, Trent dropped his Sharps and drew his pistol. He rapidly shot four more of the yelling tomahawk-waving men before one of them leaped at Trent, throwing him to the ground.

Becky screamed.

Trent held the man's hand, holding off the tomahawk long enough to put his gun barrel into the man's chest and pull the trigger. He tossed the warrior off him, rolled over, and shot the man who had his knife poised to drive into Becky's stomach.

A blast from a shotgun took out another man charging toward Becky. Trent used his last shot to drop another Comanche running toward Becky. Out of ammo, Trent dropped his Colt and grabbed his rifle as he sprung to his feet. He used the rifle to club another Comanche who charged him.

The night suddenly erupted with pistol shots. The remaining attackers dropped like flies as Pat, and Wes ran toward them, firing their pistols.

"Is that all of them?" Wes asked as he scanned the darkness beyond the wagons. *Go count*

"Becky," Trent shouted as he rushed over to the girl who lay unmoving on the ground. He kneeled beside her and touched his finger to her throat. "She's alive," he told Bruce, who fell onto his knees beside them.

Bruce pointed to his daughter's forehead. "She's got a knot."

"She must have grabbed the Comanche's hand with the tomahawk, and he hit her with his other hand," Trent said. "I think he just knocked her out."

"God, I pray that's all," Bruce said as he moved aside for Lois to have a look at her daughter.

"My baby," Lois said as she rubbed Becky's cheeks. *why?* "She glanced over at Bruce. "You and Trent carry her inside the wagon."

"I'll carry her," Trent volunteered as he scooped his hands under Becky. He grunted as he lifted her.

Bruce ran ahead and climbed into the wagon. "Hand her up to me."

Trent did as ordered and then stepped aside as Lois climbed into the wagon.

"Don't worry," Wes said as he placed his hand on Trent's shoulder. "Mama's a good nurse. Sis will be okay. I'm sure."

Trent nodded. "Okay, let's carry the dead Comanches away from the wagons so their tribe can recover the bodies.

*She rubs cheeks?*

We don't want to spark another attack by shooting men who are trying to recover the bodies of their dead."

Bruce chose some settlers to pull the bodies away from the wagons. When he finished, Trent motioned to him. "Let's walk the perimeter and calm everyone down."

"Do you think the attack is over for tonight?" Bruce asked as he waved to a woman sitting in the seat of her wagon, holding a shotgun.

"Mr. Bruce, just let one of the Comanches show his face. I'll make mush out of his head."

"I'm sure you will, Miss Carrie. Just don't go and shoot another settler," Bruce replied.

"Tomorrow afternoon, we should reach Fort Dodge. We have to take Becky to the doc right away," Trent said. "I would take her by horse tonight, but I don't think the ride would be good for her."

When they reached the halfway point around the wagons, Pat and Wes met them from the opposite direction.

"Did you see anything?" Trent asked.

"The Comanches have retrieved their dead. I didn't see any signs of aggression from them. That's doesn't mean there's not another group waiting to attack the wagons. You know how sneaky they are," Pat said.

Trent nodded. "Yup, I do. At least the moon is up. We have more light. That might help if there are more out there prepared to attack."

"Are there Comanches on the west side of Fort Dodge?" Wes asked.

"Yeah, but we'll enter Pawnee and Arapaho territories once we get out of Comanche territory. No one rides and

*Comanches are the best!*

shoots from a horse as well as an Arapaho. They're not as ferocious fighters as the Comanches and the Kiowas, but they can shoot center from a dead gallop," Pat said.

"Wow, you're a bundle of bad news," Bruce said as they reached his wagon. "Lois! How's Becky?"

Trent could tell by the expression on Lois's face that it wasn't going to be good news.

"Becky is asleep, and I can't wake her up. I'm really worried," Lois said.

"Let me have a look at her," Bruce said as he quickly climbed into the wagon.

Trent tensed when he heard Bruce calling his daughter's name over and over again without receiving a response. "Is she going to be all right?" Trent asked the moment Bruce's head appeared out of the wagon.

"We have to get her to a doctor. Let's hope we don't have any delays tomorrow and reach Fort Dodge by nightfall," Bruce said as he climbed down from the wagon.

"You'll just have to keep on pushing to reach Fort Dodge, even if it means traveling at night," Trent said. *Leave now*

Wes patted Trent on the shoulder. "Don't worry. Sis is a fighter."

Trent shook his head. "Too bad we don't have a buckboard. If we had one, I could drive her to the doc in Fort Dodge tonight." He sat beside the wagon's wheel. "Wes, you and Pat hit the bedroll. I'm going to stand guard. I can't sleep, anyway."

Wes nodded. "I'm bone tired. Fighting Comanches is tiresome." He glanced over at Pat. "Now, if I had two pistols like you, Pat, I could have killed twice as many Comanches."

"Or shot yourself in the foot," Pat said as he climbed under the wagon and unrolled his bedroll.

Wes followed Pat.

Trent heard the two talking, but his mind lingered on Becky. He blamed himself. He should have killed the Comanche before he reached Becky. It was his duty to protect the settlers, especially the Cowan family. If something happened to Becky? Trent pushed that thought out of his mind.

He hadn't been one hundred percent honest with Bruce. The range of the Comanches reached all the way to the Canadian River. The Santa Fe Trail didn't go through the panhandle of Texas. It skirted it. If Bruce were going to try to stake a claim to land in Texas, he would have to leave the wagon train and head out on his own. Trent had discussed it with Pat, but he planned on following the Cowans, wherever they decided to go. Trent's thoughts trailed off as he closed his eyes. *He's on watch — wake-up*

The vibration of the wagon wheel caused Trent's eyes to snap open. He faced east. The beauty of the first orange rays of the morning sun went unnoticed by Trent as he jumped to his feet. He turned to find Bruce climbing down from the wagon. "How is Becky?"

*guards got shot for falling asleep on guard duty!*

Bruce shook his head. "We still can't wake her. But her breathing is normal. Lois says that's a good sign."

"But is she going to be all right?" Trent demanded.

"Son, only the almighty above can answer that question, and he's not saying a word," Bruce replied. "Come on, let's get the wagons moving. Today, if a wagon breaks down, I'm not stopping. I'll have Pat and Wes stay behind to guard any wagons that have to stop for repairs."

Trent nodded. "That's a good idea. I should have thought of it already. My thinking is a little clouded. I can't stop seeing the Comanche who attacked her. I should have been able to shoot him before he reached Becky!"

Bruce shook his head. "Don't duke it out with yourself. You saved her life! Just keep that in mind, son. Now, let's get to work. We're burning daylight. The settlers are going to have to eat cold, hardtack today. We aren't going to wait until the women can cook up some vittles."

# Chapter Four
# Fort Dodge

The wagon train reached the wagon yard outside of Fort Dodge before sundown. Trent hadn't expected another wagon train at the fort, but when they arrived, a smaller one of ten wagons had taken the prime location near the river.

Bruce had constructed a stretcher from burlap bags and poles. He and Trent loaded Becky onto the stretcher, and with the help of Wes and Pat, they carried the unconscious girl inside the pine log stockade of the newly constructed fort.

Trent had expected to find log structures within the walls of the fort. Instead, he and the others were shocked to see dugouts with canvas roofs dug into the bank of the river. He figured, with all the horses in the corral they passed, the fort held at least three companies of soldiers.

Trent flagged down a soldier with several strips on his shoulder. "Sergeant, can you direct us to the post's doctor?"

"The building to the right of the boulder is the infirmary," he said, pointing to a row of dugouts.

Pat glanced at the dugouts and sod buildings. "Hmm, they built them in a hurry."

"This is the one," Trent said as he pointed to a doorway with a piece of canvas hanging from the wooden door frame to serve as a door.

They carried the stretcher into the large, damp, earthen room with a plank floor. A man in an army uniform glanced up from studying a stack of papers as they entered.

"Are you the doc?" Trent asked as he looked around for a spot to put the stretcher. He saw a table near the right wall. "Can we put her there?" he asked and nodded toward the table.

"What's wrong with her?" the middle-aged, clean-shaven man said as he adjusted his spectacles on his nose.

"A Comanche hit her on the head." Trent spoke up first.

Bruce nodded. "And she fell asleep. We can't wake her up, Doc. She's my only daughter. Please help her."

The army doctor was already moving toward the table. He nodded. "Sure, let me have a look-see. Ah, everyone but the father, please step outside and wait while I examine the girl."

Wes put his hand on Trent's shoulder. "Come on."

Trent followed him out without resisting.

"Are you folks from the big wagon train that arrived today?" a soldier asked as he stopped in front of the infirmary.

Trent shook off his mood. "Yup."

"Will y'all be taking the dry or wet trail?"

Trent looked puzzled.

"Will you stay on the Cimarron Cutoff or stick to the main trail?" the soldier rephrased the question.

"Cimarron Cutoff," Pat answered.

The soldier shook his head. "Hmm, you better be on your toes. Since the Sand Creek massacre of the Arapahos, they've allied with the Cheyenne Dog Soldiers and Comanches. They've been on a cutter. Three thousand attacked and killed twenty-nine soldiers in the Battle of Platte Bridge. Since then, the Indians have poured south all the way to Texas, attacking settlers and ranchers. The Cimarron Cutoff will be more dangerous than usual."

"How about the wet trail?" Wes asked.

The soldier shrugged. "The Apaches are on a tear too. They've been hitting every wagon on the Santa Fe Trail in the mountains. There aren't enough to hit a big wagon train head-on, but they nip at a wagon train like wolves following a buffalo herd. Either way, you take, you might lose some wagons and settlers. Good luck," he added as he hurried away.

"Well, now I can see why the army constructed the fort so hastily," Trent said. "They're trying to bring order to this region!"

"And failing," Pat said. "I would still choose the Cimarron Cutoff if I were Bruce. At least we'll see the Arapahos in the desert when they attack. You'll never see the Apaches. They'll fire from the rocks, kill a few settlers and oxen, and then disappear into the mountains, only to pop back up like prairie dogs to attack again. It's hard to defend against such attacks."

"How is Becky?" Lois said as she hurried up to the front of the infirmary. "I got here as quick as I could finish tending to the oxen."

Wes shook his head. "Sorry you had to do that alone, *he should have done it & let her go*
Ma." *With Becky*

"I didn't. Ralf helped. Anyway, getting Becky to the doctor was more urgent." Lois paused. "Any word from the doctor?"

Trent shook his head. "He shooed us out. He only let Bruce stay."

"Then I best go on inside and see what's going on with my daughter," Lois said as she pushed aside the canvas curtain and entered the infirmary.

Once his mother entered the infirmary, Wes glanced at Trent and shook his head. "This seems to be a bad year to be on the Santa Fe Trail."

Trent nodded. "I reckon."

"No," Pat disagreed. "The Comanches and Arapahos and Apaches have been causing trouble for settlers heading west for years. This year is no different."

"We're going to be exposed to raids on either trail, but if we take the Cimarron Cutoff, we'll shorten the exposure by ten days," Trent pointed out.

Seeing movement at the door of the infirmary, everyone turned to look. Bruce pushed aside the curtain. He glanced directly at Trent and smiled. "Becky is awake and sitting up, talking to her mother," he announced. "The doctor says she'll be fine."

Trent jerked off his Boss of the Plains hat and slapped it against his leg. "Dang it! That's great! Can I see her?"

Bruce shook his head. "No, the doctor wanted Lois to feed her and then let her rest in the infirmary until tomorrow." *She'd be better out in the air — not in a hole in the bank —*

"Oh," Trent said and sounded disappointed.

"Come on, Trent," Pat said. "I spotted a cantina just outside the fort. Let's all go there for a shot of whiskey."

"You fellows go on and relax over a few drinks. I'm going to rustle up some vittles for Becky. Then I'll head back to the wagon train to see if everything is all right." *Still isnt helping like a son Should*

Lobo sat, waiting for Trent outside the gate. He wagged his tail and fell in behind Trent as he, Pat, and Wes headed for the Outpost Cantina. The saloon occupied an adobe building that looked hastily built, like everything else about the fort. The men sitting at tables and the bar could be identified by their clothes as settlers and well-armed wagon train scouts.

Several of the settlers sitting at the table they passed on their way to the bar bristled when they spotted Pat. The bartender, a chubby man with a gray beard and beady eyes, shook his head at the three as they approached the bar. He eyed Pat and Lobo.

"We don't want no Indians or dogs!" he said with his arms crossed over his chest.

Trent, still in a bad mood about not being able to see Becky, didn't take the bartender's words kindly. "We don't give a rat's fart what you want or don't want, mister." He shifted the buffalo rifle in the crook of his arm.

The closest man to Trent, a scout wearing a buckskin shirt that smelled of sweat and horsehair, turned to face Trent. "You'd best listen to what Daniel says..."

Trent brought the butt of the rifle up in a lightning-quick move. The stock of the buffalo rifle struck the man under the jaw. The scout dropped to the floor like a sack of potatoes.

Trent looked around the room. "Anyone else have any objections to us drinking whiskey?"

Pat squared his shoulders to the bar and glared at the bartender. He touched his fingers to the handles of his Colt Navies. "You reach for that scattergun, and it will be the last thing you reach for, friend."

The bartender took a step back and lifted his hands. "I don't want any fuss with you men."

"Then you best start pouring whiskey," Trent called out.

The bartender turned around and grabbed three shot glasses and a bottle filled with a reddish liquid.

"That's better," Trent said. Trent glanced down at the man he had struck with the stock of his rifle. "Somebody help the man up and sit him in a chair before my dog decides he's dinner.

A couple of men also dressed in buckskin shirts from farther down the bar walked over and carried the unconscious man to a table, set him in a chair, and leaned his head on the table.

"Are y'all from that big wagon train?" a man in a dirty blue shirt and slouch hat called out. He sat at a table where he shared a bottle of whiskey with three other rough-looking men.

"Yup!" Trent said as he lifted the shot of whiskey and tossed it down. "Dang, that is firewater!" He glanced over at Pat. "I guess you like it?"

"Of course," Pat said with a straight face as he drank his whiskey.

"Did y'all have Comanche trouble?"

No we gave them whiskey & a gun!

"We did, but we sent them packing," Wes said as he held his glass of whiskey up as though getting up enough courage to drink it. "They don't like sharpshooters with buffalo rifles. Or a Yaqui packing two pistols."

"Well," the man said. "You ain't out of the woods. It's worse west of the fort. There's a river crossing the Indians use. The Santa Fe Trail runs right through it. You ain't likely to get far from the fort before you attract the attention of Indians, be they Comanches, Pawnees, or Arapaho dog eaters."

Wes choked on his whiskey. "They eat dogs?"

"Yup," Trent said. He glanced down at Lobo. "And wolves," he added.

The man rose from the table. He took a step toward Trent, only to find Lobo suddenly between him and Trent, growling.

"He's protective," Trent said.

"Yeah, so I see," the man said as he went back to his chair. "How many guards do you have for your wagon train?"

Pat turned from the bar and looked directly in the man's eyes, "Enough to deal with Comanches and bandits."

The man smiled. However, the smile didn't touch his eyes as he glared at Pat. The man poured himself a shot of whiskey. "You look like an Indian but don't sound like one."

"You look and sound like a bandit," Pat said. "You've got blood spatters on your boots. You should clean them after a raid."

The man looked at Pat's two pistols and smiled. "Killed a mule deer. Guess I got some blood on my shoe."

Pat shook his head. "I don't smell deer blood." He nodded at the man's Colt Army. "I smell gunpowder. Didn't know folks hunted mule deer with a pistol."

The man tensed for a moment, then relaxed and forced his smile back in place. "I had to make sure he was dead. I didn't want to get gored."

"If you say so, pardner," Pat said dismissively. He turned his back on the man but watched him in the mirror behind the bar.

"I guess we better ride on back to our camp, boys," the man said as he slowly rose from his chair. The three men at his table stood, as did the four men at the next table, and they followed the man in the blue shirt.

Trent nodded. "Let's hope we don't meet again."

Wes waited until the men walked through the butterfly doors, then he said, "Do you really think he's a bandit, Pat?"

"Yup," Pat said as he continued to lean against the bar. "He rode to the fort to check out the wagon trains to see if there might be some easy pickings heading out soon."

"And you could tell this by the blood on his boots?" Wes asked.

"That and the spider tattoo on his gun hand. He's a bandit out of Texas named Sam Good. He's wanted by the Texas Rangers and every other lawman in Texas."

"Does he have a bounty on his head?" Wes asked.

"Yup, and a big one." Trent spoke up. "Pat, I missed the spider tattoo on his gun hand."

"You're distracted. You are still thinking about Becky," Pat said.

"Why don't we collect the bounty on him?" Wes asked.

on track mind —

"A couple of the men at the second table had their holsters tilted toward us and their fingers on the triggers. I didn't want you catching a bullet, Wes. Your old man would skin us alive if Trent and I got you shot in a saloon brawl. And as I've told you before, Trent and I are not bounty hunters."

# Chapter Five
# Isaiah Moses & his
# Wagon Train

Trent watched as the ten-wagon train of a preacher named Isiah Moses pulled slowly away from the fort. The wagon master had declined Bruce's invitation to join his larger wagon train.

The wagon master, Lee Cobb, hadn't wanted to be slowed down by the slower oxen teams. So even though a smaller wagon train encouraged attacks, Mr. Cobb had chosen speed over safety. Preacher Moses had supported the wagon master he had hired by telling Bruce the Lord would protect them from the heathens.

Trent hoped the wagon master had made the correct choice. However, he feared ill would come from the religious sect not joining Bruce's wagon train.

Wes joined Trent. "Why is Mr. Cobb in such a hurry to get to California?"

"I guess he leads wagons to California for a living. The sooner he gets there, the sooner he can return to lead another wagon train."

"I didn't see any pistols or rifles carried by the men on the wagon train, only a few shotguns," Wes added. "I'm wondering how they have made it this far."

Trent shrugged. "Preacher Moses said the Lord would protect them. Hmm, maybe he has."

Wes touched his Peacemaker. "I prefer to trust my Colt instead of prayer during a Comanche attack."

Pat walked up to join them. "Trent, Lois is bringing Becky to the wagon."

Trent turned and hurried toward the Cowans' wagon. He arrived in time to see Becky walking gingerly beside her mother as they approached their wagon.

"Becky," Trent called out as he approached the two women with Lobo beside him.

Becky smiled weakly. "Hi."

"How are you feeling?" Trent asked as he walked alongside her. Lobo glanced up at Becky and whined.

"Shaky. I just want to get in the wagon and lie down," Becky replied as she ignored Lobo.

"Yeah, sure thing. I'll come by later to see how you are," Trent said as he dropped back to watch Becky and Lois as they made their way to their wagon, where Bruce awaited them.

"Sis is still all shaken up from the attack. I heard Ma tell Pa she woke up screaming several times during the night. But don't worry, she'll be back to her ornery self in no time," Wes said. *Too Bad —*

Trent waited until Becky disappeared inside the wagon before he approached Bruce.

"I guess we can head out, Trent," Bruce said.

"Did Wes tell you what happened in the saloon?" Trent asked.

"He mentioned you knocked a man senseless with the butt of your rifle. Was there something else that happened?"

Trent nodded. "Yeah, I had a not-too-friendly chat with Sam Good in the saloon."

Bruce shrugged. "Who is Sam Good? Should I know him?"

"He's wanted for massacring settlers in Texas. He has a big bounty on his head. Word has it he's moved up and is hitting the wagon trains on the Santa Fe Trail."

"What it is with all these bandits riding up from Texas?" Bruce asked.

"The Texas Rangers!" Trent said. "They're making it too hot in Texas for gangs of bandits like Sam Good's. The Texas Rangers are relentless, worse than bounty hunters about shooting first and asking questions later."

"If he is a wanted man, how did they just waltz into Fort Dodge?"

Trent shrugged. "This isn't Texas. His face isn't well known. But I stopped by and reported seeing him to the commander of the fort. He didn't seem to take much stock in what I had to say. Guess he's up to his ears in Comanches and Pawnees and can't worry about a bandit from Texas."

"Why do you think this Sam Good fellow visited the fort?"

"To see if there are any easy pickings heading along the Santa Fe Trail... that's my guess."

Bruce shook his head. "If Sam Good spotted Preacher Moses's wagon train, I guess they're riding into trouble. Did you mention this Sam Good gent to Mr. Cobb?"

"Nah, he had his mind made up. I would have just been blowing air. And the preacher believes the Lord will take care of his flock."

"Well, Trent, let's hope someone is looking after their welfare better than Mr. Cobb." Bruce paused and glanced around. "I guess you can give the orders to head out?"

"Where's Marty and Grace Jones and your second wagon?" Trent asked. "I haven't seen them since we arrived at the fort."

"They didn't want to continue. They're staying at the fort. And I sold the oxen and the wagon."

"What about the supplies in the wagon?" STUPID!

Bruce shrugged. "I sold what supplies I couldn't carry in the wagon." Bruce motioned to the rear of the wagon where four horses were tied. "I bought two extra horses. One for Lois and me in case something happens to the oxen."

"Four horses could pull the wagon," Trent said.

"If push comes to shove, I guess we can hitch them up with Wes and Becky's horses."

Trent shook his head. "Let's hope we don't have to do that." He patted Lobo on the head. "Come on, let's get the wagons rolling."

It took Trent and Pat an hour to get all the wagons moving. From a distance, the wagon train looked like a long, disjointed snake slowly crawling across the flat plains. Late afternoon found them in sight of distant hills that cut the monotony of the sea of waving grass.

"Have you talked to Sis any more?" Wes asked while he and Trent rode point.

"I stopped by the wagon, but Miss Lois said Becky didn't feel up to a visitor," Trent said with a little sadness in his voice. "She had a darn bad experience. It's going to take her a while to get over it," he added.

"Yeah, I guess she came as close to death as one can get," Wes said. "You saved my sister's life, Trent. And I thank you for that. Pa and Ma would be heartbroken if something happened to Becky. She is the apple of their eye."

Trent shook his head. "I should have kill't that warrior before he got to Becky. Her getting hurt is my fault." Lobo, who trotted alongside Trent, let out a yip.

"Here comes Pat from the rear," Wes said.

Trent turned in the saddle as his brother slowed Leo to a walk. "Don't tell me we have a broken wagon wheel already."

"Nope, Bruce wants to know if we should try to reach the hills or stop on the flats."

Trent smiled. "He's learning. The hills could provide cover for bushwhackers." He turned around to face Wes. "You ride back and tell your pa we'll stop before the hills. And then ride back up and take point. Pat and I need to scout ahead to make sure they're no surprises waiting for us in the hills."

"Sure thing, Trent," Wes said as he whipped his Quarter Horse around and galloped toward the rear of the wagon train.

"The kid sure has grown up since we met him," Pat said. "He's going to make a good man."

"If he lives long enough. He's reckless, Pat. And it's going to get him killed if he's not careful." *or some one else killed — like Pat —*

"Don't worry, I'll watch after him," Pat said while they trotted their horses toward the hills.

"I'm worried about Becky... She seems remote. She hasn't spoken to me since she got in the wagon," Trent confessed as they approached the summit of the first hill. *Should be—by now—*

"She's still in shock. She's not used to violence. Don't forget she grew up in Boston and not out west. After all the killing she's seen since she arrived in Kansas City, I'm surprised she hasn't crawled into a shell like a turtle before now," Pat said as they topped the summit.

"Yup, you are..." The words died in Trent's throat.

Before them lay ten abandoned wagons. Unmoving forms of men, women, and children lay sprawled in the trampled grass among the wagons. Trent and Pat exchanged looks.

"Sam Good!" Trent said the name as though it were a curse. "I should have put him in the dirt in the saloon."

Pat shook his head. "No, you might have gotten Wes killed. His men had us covered."

"Yeah, but look what happened. These folks weren't even armed. Yet Sam shot them all. I just hope they killed that Cobb fellow too. He deserves it for being so reckless."

"Well, let's ride down and see if he's among the dead," Pat said as he urged Leo into a trot.

Trent pressed his knees into Tex's sides, and the big stallion trotted after Pat. He kept shaking his head as they rode past the bodies. Anger built up inside him until he thought his head would explode. The killing had been senseless. Sam Good could have easily robbed the settlers of all their valuables and horses without massacring everyone.

Lobo moved from body to body, sniffing. After he finished his investigation, he walked up beside Tex, looked up at Trent, and whined.

Trent nodded at Pat. "Ain't nobody alive."

"Did you spot Cobb among the dead?" Pat asked.

Trent shook his head. "Nope. And that's peculiar. Sam Good wouldn't have left the wagon master alive. And did you notice the wagon with the busted wheel? And that some settlers were shot in the back while running away from the wagons?" *unless he's working with Sam Good !*

"I smell a skunk. I saw them settlers checking their wagons. They would have spotted a wheel that needed attention." *wow — what gave you that idea ?*

"Yup, I'm thinking the same thing. I bet Cobb was in on the raid. He refused to join Bruce's wagon train so he could set Preacher Moses's wagons up for the ambush. He might even have had something to do with the busted wheel." Trent agreed, "Cobb killed some settlers when the attack started."

"I'm wondering how many times Sam Good has sent one of his men to Fort Dodge pretending to be a wagon master," Pat said.

Trent nodded. "Well, now we know why he had to kill everyone. He couldn't leave any witnesses."

"You think they'll try to hit us?"

"No, we have too many armed men. He'll probably wait in the area to repeat the trick with another smaller wagon train that passes through Fort Dodge. If they already have a wagon master, he'll try to attach one of his men as a scout or guard.

"I guess we should ride back and tell Bruce. He'll want to bury the dead settlers before the women folk see them," Pat said.

"Yup. Let's head back. Nothing more we can do here," Trent said as he reined Tex around. "Come on, Lobo."

Wes rode out to meet them. He saw the expression on Trent's face. "Is something wrong?"

"It's Preacher Moses's wagon train. Looks like Sam Good ambushed them. Everyone's dead," Trent said.

"Dang it. We should have put him in the dirt when we had the chance! Trent, this is on our shoulders," Wes said. He held Trent's gaze for a moment. "We have to make it right."

"Yup and we will, but we have graves to dig first," Trent said as he kneed Tex. "Well, let's get back to the rear and tell Bruce the bad news."

"Pa's going to be fit to be tied," Wes said.

"He's going to like even worse what I'm going to do," Trent mumbled when his big stallion broke into a canter.

Bruce, trudging alongside his lead oxen, shook his head when Trent approached at a fast gallop. "What in the blazes now?"

Trent waited until Tex slowed down to a walk and turned him to keep pace with Bruce as Wes and Pat joined them. "Bandits raided Preacher Moses's wagon train," Trent said.

"Anyone hurt?"

"Everyone is dead, Pa," Wes called out. "We think Sam Good massacred the entire wagon train."

Bruce pulled off his bowler hat and slapped it against his leg. "Even the children?"

never hear about the baby they are taking care of — from Book 1

Trent nodded. "Yup, everyone."

Bruce shook his head. "Why?"

"Pa, the wagon master betrayed the wagon train. Pat thinks he disabled a wagon to set up the attack."

Bruce glanced at Pat. "Is that right? Was Mr. Cobb complicit?"

"By my reckoning, Cobb is a member of the Sam Good gang," Pat replied.

"We think Sam put him on a wagon train to help with the raids. He killed everyone to keep it secret that Cobb helped. And Cobb probably shot some settlers." Trent rubbed his horse's neck, trying to soothe his own nerves.

"May they burn in Hell!"

"What's the matter?" Lois called out from the seat of the wagon. She looked surprised at her husband's curse.

"Bandits hit Preacher Moses's wagons. Lois, they killed even the children."

Lois put her hands over her mouth. "Lord, have mercy on us! Satan walks among us for sure."

"Not Satan. A man called Sam Good. Pat and I are going to make Sam and his gang pay the piper," Trent said.

"What do you mean by that?" Bruce asked.

"My brother and I are going after the gang. I should have put him in the dirt in the saloon. What happened to the wagon train is on me," Trent said.

"I'm going with them, Pa," Wes called out.

Pat shook his head. "No, you are staying here to protect your family. Trent and I might be gone for a couple of days. There are more bandits than just Sam Good's gang waiting to pounce on a wagon train. And we're still in Comanche country."

"Pat's right, Wes. Your pistol might be needed here. And I want to make sure Becky is protected while I'm away."

Wes reluctantly nodded. "Okay, Trent. But don't return before you put a bullet in Sam Good and Cobb."

now a 15 year old is giving orders — a green 15 year old boy —

# Chapter Six
# The Man with
# the Spider Tattoo

*P 37—on his gun hand*

Pat glanced up at Trent, mounted on Tex. "Nine horses."

"That the number I figured it would be. Seven men were in the cantina with Sam at the fort. Then Cobb joined them after the raid."

"We've faced worse odds," Pat said after he mounted his spotted mustang. "Of course, it would be better if I hadn't had to give up my Sharps to that Comanche war chief."

"Ah, you can't shoot center with a Sharps anyway," Trent teased.

Pat ignored Trent's remark. "They have several hours head start on us. I think they'll run to ground. They probably have a hideout not far from the trail."

Lobo sniffed the horse tracks and growled.

"He doesn't like Sam Good," Trent said. "I think if you lose their track, Lobo might be able to follow their scent."

"If they're headed into the rocky foothills, it might come down to Lobo tracking them. I can track across rocks, but it's time-consuming."

"You know, Becky didn't want me to come into the wagon to see her before we started after Sam's gang."

"Why?" Pat asked.

"Bruce said she got upset when she heard about the massacre."

Pat nodded. "Everyone did."

"Yeah, but she also seems upset at me too."

"She'll be back to taking long rides with you, Trent. Give her some time." *you'll get over it — & better off*

"I hope you're right. I just hope you are right." *without the spoiled brat*

The prairie changed from flat to rolling hills. By the late afternoon, the hills became littered with rocks and large boulders. Mountains loomed before them by the time the sun hung low on the horizon.

"I've lost their trail," Pat proclaimed as he bent down to study the rocky ground that was too hard packed for grass to grow. The only greenery was patches of beggar weeds and thistles, and even they grew so close to the rocks that the hooves of the horses hadn't disturbed them. Pat climbed back on his mustang. "What do we do now?"

Trent pointed at Lobo. The big wolf-dog walked ahead of them with his nose close to the ground. "We follow him."

"He could be sniffing out a mule deer," Pat said.

"Maybe, but he's all we got, and he's heading in the direction the tracks have been going for the past couple of hours."

Pat shrugged. "Okay. I guess it's follow him or turn back."

Since Pat didn't have to walk, they proceeded at a trot. Lobo seemed sure of the trail he followed. They were in the shadow of the mountains when Trent held up his hand. "I smell smoke."

"Yup, me too," Pat said. "There's an opening to a canyon yonder. It could be that's their hideout. Maybe they have a shack in the canyon."

Trent nodded. "Let's dismount."

Lobo walked toward the canyon.

"Lobo, come here," Trent called out as he patted his leg. The big wolf-dog turned back immediately.

"So what's the plan?"

"Well, we can't just ride into the canyon. If Sam Good is smart, and I haven't heard otherwise, he'll have a guard posted on the wall of the canyon."

Pat nodded. "I guess one of us is going to have to play mountain goat."

"Yup, and since your pistols lack the range, I'll have to be the goat."

"Well, you sort of look like one, anyway."

"You keep jawing at me like that, and I'll give you the Sharps and you can shimmy up the rocks."

"Nah... you know you wouldn't give me your Sharps. Hell, sometimes I think you care for the buffalo rifle more than you do Becky."

"I've known my rifle longer," Trent said as he looped Tex's reins around a rock. He pulled a long piece of rawhide out of his saddlebags and tied it to the barrel and stock of his rifle. He slung it over his shoulder. "Lobo, you stay." Trent took a step toward the wall of the canyon. "Pat, when you hear me fire, get on your mustang and ride into the canyon with guns blazing."

Pat nodded.

Trent took a deep breath before he started to climb the rocks alongside the canyon. He hated climbing. Pat could climb like a goat. However, his brother's skills with a rifle couldn't match his, so the job of eliminating the guard and picking off Sam's men from a distance fell to him.

To make matters worse, Trent had to navigate the rocks while he made little to no noise. If a guard got the drop on him while he climbed to the top of the canyon's wall, he would be as good as dead.

The light had started to fail by the time Trent reached the top of the canyon's wall. That fact saved his life. The guard sat facing him, twenty yards away, when Trent glanced over the rim of the canyon.

Trent now faced a dilemma: if he shot the guard, he would alert the gang to his presence. When Pat rode in, they would be ready for him and, more than likely, put his brother in the dirt. He had to dispatch the guard with his knife. The guard facing his direction presented a problem.

Trent glanced around the ledge for a small rock. After a few minutes, he found one small enough to do the trick—at least he hoped it would. Moving back to the rim of the canyon, Trent tossed the stone over the head of the guard. He waited until he heard the rock hit before he peeked over the rim.

The guard had sprung to his feet and turned in the direction of the sound. Trent waited until the guard walked a couple of paces in the opposite direction before he quietly climbed on to the canyon's wall. As he crept after the guard, he pulled his big knife and held it ready.

Trent approached within four feet of the guard before the man sensed his presence. He turned, but not quick enough. Trent covered the distance between them, and then as the man turned to face him, Trent sliced the man's throat with a move that cut deep into the flesh.

The guard dropped his rifle and reached for his throat. He tried in vain to stop the blood from squirting between his fingers as he crumpled to the ground.

"That's for the children you slaughtered," Trent hissed.

Trent drew the guard's Colt Army but left the man's rifle where it had fallen. He didn't need the rifle, but he might need another pistol before the gunplay ended.

"Okay," Trent mumbled. "Let's see what you are protecting."

He had to walk almost to the end of the canyon before he spotted the adobe shack. From the looks of the corral, Sam had been using the cabin as a hideout for quite a while. A well had been dug in front. With water and supplies, the gang could hold out here for months if the law was too hot on their trail.

Through the front window, Trent could see men sitting at a table eating by the light of a lantern. Trent squinted his eyes as he tried to identify Sam Good. He didn't spot the man. Trent figured he probably sat at the other end of the table. However, he did recognize Cobb. Trent gritted his teeth in anger as he pulled the Sharps off his shoulder.

Trent lay prone at the edge of the canyon and took careful aim through the window at Cobb. The former wagon master sat at the end of the table, a place usually reserved for men of importance. As Cobb lifted his fork to his mouth,

Trent fired. The explosive sound echoed from the canyon walls like thunder as Cobb's face fell forward onto his plate.

Before the echoes of the buffalo rifle died, Trent had reloaded. One of the outlaws ran out the front door. The sound of the buffalo rifle reverberated in the canyon again. The exposed outlaw grabbed his chest and pitched backward into the shack.

Figuring no one else would be stupid enough to run out, Trent turned his aim to the window. He spotted the right half of the face of one of the outlaws as the man tried to locate him. "Pat wouldn't have been able to make this shot," Trent mumbled as he squeezed the trigger. The man fell.

Knowing that Pat would ride in, Trent aimed his next shot a foot right of the window. He fired with confidence that the buffalo rifle could penetrate the adobe wall of the shack. He didn't know if he had hit anyone, but he felt sure he had put the fear of the devil in them. He waited to see if any of the outlaws would show their faces when they heard Pat's horse.

He didn't have to wait long. Pat, riding low in the saddle with both pistols drawn, rode up to the cabin like the grim reaper. One of the outlaws couldn't resist glancing through the window. Trent put him in the dirt as Pat leaped off his horse and took cover behind the well while he fired his pistols.

Pat turned and motioned to Trent that he intended to rush the shack. Trent waved back and immediately looked down the sights of his rifle. A moment before Pat sprung to his feet, Trent saw the door to the shack start to swing open.

He shot into the door and saw it slam shut as though someone had fallen against it.

By the time Pat reached the wall of the adobe building next to the door, Trent had reloaded and swung his sights to cover the window, just in time to see a man reach out with a pistol, intent on shooting his brother in the back. The outlaw died without completing his desire.

Trent heard someone call out from inside the shack but couldn't tell what the outlaw said. Pat answered the man. A moment later, the door of the cabin slowly opened. Someone threw a pistol onto the ground. Then Sam Good stepped out with his hands over his head. Pat tensed.

Trent thought his brother would shoot the outlaw in cold blood. The thought might have been running through Pat's mind. However, he finally shouted something, and Sam turned his back to Pat. Trent's brother stepped forward and struck the outlaw in the back of the head with the handle of his right pistol. Sam Good crumpled to the ground.

When Trent climbed down the way he had come, he found Lobo sitting next to Tex, waiting for him. The big dog rushed to Trent and almost knocked him down as he licked him in the face. "Okay, that's enough. Let's help Pat with Sam Good."

By the time Trent rode up to the shack, Pat had Sam's hands tied behind his back and laid out on the ground.

"I should have killed you and your brother in the cantina," Sam said in a Texan drawl.

"Funny, I've been thinking I should have killed you too. If I had, I would have saved the lives of those in the wagon train," Trent said. He nodded at his brother. "What are you going to do with him?"

"I'm going to take him and his men back to Fort Dodge and collect the reward," Pat said, and surprising Trent.

"You're going to collect the bounty on him and his gang?"

"Yup," Pat said.

"Are you going to turn into a bounty hunter?" Trent demanded.

"We can use that money. Don't try to change my mind. I've made it up. I'm turning him and his men in for the reward. You ride on back to the wagon train. I'll catch up with you when I'm finished."

Trent nodded. "Okay, if that's how you want to play it. Do you need help to tie the dead men on their horses?"

Pat shook his head. "No, you head back to the wagon train. You might catch up with them by daylight. I'll stack the bodies in the shack and head out at first light for Fort Dodge."

Trent mounted Tex. "Come on, Lobo, let's head back!" he shouted before reining the big stallion around and trotting toward the mouth of the canyon.

mistake!

# Chapter Seven
# The Cimarron Cutoff

Trent reined Tex to a stop beside Bruce's horse. He surveyed the trail below, noting how it forked north and south. Trent nodded over at Bruce. "Well, this is your final chance to take the mountain branch."

Bruce shook his head. "Nope, I've made up my mind. We'll take the Cimarron Cutoff. All the wagons have an extra barrel for water. We should make it through the dry part of the trail. I've heard there are a few watering holes in the desert."

Trent nodded. "Yup, but they're unreliable. If they're dry, we'll run out of water before we get to the Canadian River."

"Let's pray they aren't dry."

Trent shook his head. "I don't put much stock in prayer to avoid trouble. I'll stick to knowhow and information. Isn't there a saying? The Lord helps those who help themselves."

"We'll just have to risk it, Trent. Some settlers barely have enough supplies to get to Santa Fe. If we take the mountain route, they'll run out of food days before we reach Santa Fe."

"Boss, I hear you. I just thought it was my duty to point out the dangers of the Cimarron Cutoff, and I have."

"I see your brother caught up with us last night. Wes told me he took Sam Good back to Fort Dodge for the bounty on him and his men," Bruce said in a disapproving tone.

"Yup, and he's loaded with Lincolns! I fear that, in the future, he and Wes might take to bounty-hunting."

"Yeah, I've noticed Pat and my son are getting thicker than thieves. I believe whatever Pat decides to do at the end of the trail, Wes will join him."

"My brother is old enough to make up his mind what he wants to do with his life. I ain't going to try to persuade him otherwise if he turns to bounty-hunting. However, it's something that I'm not a mind to do."

"And just what do you have in mind to do after the wagon train?"

"I've a mind to find me a nice piece of land and homestead it," Trent replied.

"How are things going with you and Becky?" Bruce asked.

Trent shrugged. "She won't leave the wagon to go for a ride. She's always reading and hardly talks to me."

"That Comanche almost killed Becky. She still has nightmares about the attack. But she'll get back to her old self soon. Just be patient with her."

"I'll wait for her as long as it takes."

Bruce smiled. "I'm glad to hear that, Trent."

Trent nodded. "Thanks. Now, I better make my rounds and check the wagon. We have to ford the Arkansas River this afternoon. I want to make sure there are no problems with the wagons. I hear the crossing can be dangerous."

"I don't like crossing rivers. A lot of things can go wrong," Bruce said.

"There ain't no way around it, I'm afraid," Trent said. "But by hook or by crook, Pat and I will get all the wagons safely across the Arkansas."

"That's what I want to hear, son," Bruce called after Trent as he went in search of his brother.

Trent found his brother sitting on Leo, studying the hills north of the trail. He stopped Tex alongside of Leo. "Is something wrong?"

"Yup, I spotted an Arapaho shadowing the wagon train," Pat said while he continued to stare at the hills.

"Just one?"

Pat nodded. "But there's more, I'm sure. The dog eaters don't do anything alone."

Trent glanced down at Lobo. "You hear that, Lobo. Dog eaters are nearby. You better stay close to me, or you'll end up over a cooking fire."

"Since the Sand Creek massacre, the Arapaho have been killing every white man they come across," Pat said.

"So are they going to attack?" Trent asked.

"They aren't going to let the wagons just pass through their territory without some form of confrontation," Pat said.

Trent nodded. "If they're going to attack the wagon train, it'll be while we're fording the Arkansas."

"Yup, that's what I'm thinking too."

Trent shook his head. "I hate to tell Bruce. He ain't going to take the news of another attack kindly."

"At least the Arapaho aren't as bad as the Comanche," Pat said.

"Tell that to Lobo," Trent said before he kneed Tex and headed back to report the news to Bruce.

Bruce glanced up while he tied his horse to the back of the wagon. "What now?"

"Arapaho!" Trent said.

"What about them? Are they going to attack my wagon train?"

"Pat thinks it's possible, well, likely. They're in dire straits. They've been attacked by the Comanches and Kiowas and pushed from their territories. With the decline of the buffalo herds and their lost crops, they're starving."

"I didn't know they were farmers," Bruce said.

"The Arapaho and some other tribes are part-time farmers," Trent replied. "My mother's people, the Yaqui, were farmers," he added. "However, don't take that to mean they don't know how to fight. The Arapaho are fierce warriors."

"So what do we do? Do we stop and circle the wagons?"

"No, we keep on, but if they plan on attacking, it'll be at the river crossing."

"So what's the plan?"

"They'll attack from this side of the river. I'll have most of the men guard the wagons as they approach the crossing. I'll also have several teams of men to help the women drive the oxen across."

"How far are we from the river crossing?" Bruce asked.

"About two hours. I sent Pat ahead to check out the area to see if anyone might be planning an ambush." Trent shrugged. "Maybe we'll be luckier than a bear finding honey and they won't attack."

Bruce pointed up the trail. "Hmm, isn't that Pat riding like the devil?" He shook his head. "If he's riding that hard, it can't be good news."

Trent nodded. "Yup, it can't be good."

Neither of the men spoke as Pat reined in his mustang to a stop in front of Trent and Bruce. They all stared at each other.

Bruce shook his head. "Pat, I don't think I want to hear what you have to say."

"Nope, you ain't going to like it."

"Well, tell me anyway."

"At least seventy Arapaho warriors are blocking the crossing. Most are armed with rifles and pistols."

"Dang it!" Bruce yelled.

"What do you think they want? Why block the crossing instead of setting an ambush?" Trent asked.

"I'm guessing they want us to pay tribute to cross," Pat replied.

"What kind of tribute?" Bruce asked.

"Horses, guns, ammo, or barrels of flour, I'm guessing."

"Hmm," Bruce said. "Most of the settlers have at least one horse or mule trailing their wagons. We have extra guns, but flour we need."

"So you want to try to trade with them?" Pat asked.

"What I don't want is to get any of the settlers killed. I think they'll agree to give up a horse or one of their spare rifles or pistols if it means avoiding a fight. But I guess we have to know what their demands are before we can make the decision," Bruce replied.

Trent nodded. "Pat and I will ride to the crossing and parley with them. In the meantime, keep the wagons moving but have everyone carry a gun."

"I'll send Wes around to warn the settlers," Bruce said as he spotted his son riding toward them. "Y'all go and negotiate. If they ask too much to cross, tell them we'll fight. I can't strip the settlers of supplies to the point they can't survive the rest of the trip."

Without a word, Trent and Pat whipped their mounts around and urged them into a gallop. They rode hard until they approached the line of warriors stretched out along the bank of the Arkansas River.

Trent glanced over at his brother. "Do you know their language?"

"Nope, I'll have to use sign language."

Trent shifted his Sharps in the crook of his arm. "Just be ready if things get ugly." He glanced down at Lobo. "Make sure you tell them my dog isn't for the stew pot."

"Hmm, he's big enough to feed the entire lodge."

"I'm going to shoot the first one that licks his chops," Trent said half-jokingly.

"If you do that, there might not be enough left to parley with," Pat said with a straight face.

Trent shook his head but didn't comment as they neared the line of Arapahos. A warrior wearing a war bonnet of eagle feathers rode out to meet them. Trent hung back to let Pat parley with the chief alone.

The two exchanged greeting signs, but after that, Trent lost the conversation. He hadn't bothered to learn the sign language. Pat had always been at his side when they had been forced to communicate with the different tribes.

As Pat and the chief exchanged signs, Trent looked over the warriors. Most of them appeared well armed with rifles or pistols. He found it amusing that those with pistols wore them in holsters on a cartridge belt, the same as he and Pat.

Trent counted seventy-five mounted Arapaho. Most of the warriors appeared to be his age or younger. Although slim, they all seemed to be healthy. If it came to a fight, the settlers would be facing a new crop of warriors eager to prove their bravery. Both sides would have casualties.

Finally, the war chief wheeled his pony around and rode back to the line of warriors. Trent waited impatiently for Pat to reach him and report.

"Well?" Trent called out as Pat rode into earshot.

Pat waited to reply until he stopped Leo beside Tex. "Two Moons doesn't want to fight but will if we don't meet his demands."

"And what are they?"

"He wants twenty horses and ten rifles," Pat said.

"That's steep."

"He's willing to send twenty of his warriors to escort the wagons to the Canadian River. Those warriors will be given our horses. The rifles he will take," Pat explained.

Trent nodded. "So he's short of horses for his new crop of warriors. And he's sending them out to test their courage if the wagons run into trouble between the Arkansas and the Canadian. That's a smart move."

"Do you think Bruce will agree?"

"Yup, neither he nor the settlers want another fight on their hands. Go back and tell the chief we agree."

"Don't you want to discuss it with Bruce?" Pat asked.

"Nope, this is a decision we're better able to make. Bruce is learning, but he's still not smart about dealing with the tribes. That's our job."

"Okay, I'll go tell Chief Two Moons."

"While you're jawing with the war chief, I'll head back and break the news to Bruce. If he's going to cuss and yell, it should be at me and not you."

Pat nodded and spun Leo around like a cutting horse and galloped back toward the line of warriors.

Trent glanced down at Lobo. "Lobo, you might have to protect me from Bruce when I tell him the deal I made."

Trent found Bruce sitting on his horse at the head of the wagon train when he rode back. The wagon master wore a grim expression. "Tell me the bad news!"

"It ain't all bad. We made a deal with Two Moons, the war chief."

"What did he demand, our firstborn?"

Trent shook his head. "Not quite."

"Then what?"

"Twenty horses and ten rifles."

Bruce didn't answer immediately. "That's steep just to cross the river. But then we could lose that many horses in a fight and some oxen too."

"And also some settlers," Trent added.

"Yep, that's right. But we're going to need the rifles if we run into any more scuffles before we get to Santa Fe."

"Yup, but the chief will send twenty young warriors to escort us to the Canadian River. They'll ride the horses we're handing over to the war chief," Trent explained.

"Can we trust his men not to kill us in our sleep?" Bruce asked.

"The Arapaho are traders as well as farmers. They're proud people and take great pride in sticking to an agreement. Honor will bind the warriors to assists us in any fight," Trent said. "They're being sent to prove their bravery."

Bruce shrugged. "Well, if you say it's a good agreement, I'm fine with it."

"Good, I'll go around the wagons and tell the settlers to put away their guns. I don't want one of them to get trigger happy and shoot one of the warriors. If that happens, all Hell will break loose."

Later, Trent and Wes led the twenty horses up to the group of waiting men. They also carried the ten rifles in two burlap bags. Two Moons waited with another Arapaho warrior beside Pat to take the rifles.

The chief spoke to the twenty waiting young Arapaho men. When he finished, he signed to Pat.

"Trent, he instructed the men to select their horses," Pat said as the young Arapahos moved among the string of horses, patting and stroking them.

"They all look mighty wet behind the ears to be full-fledged warriors," Trent said.

"None have counted crop. They aren't warriors yet. Two Moons hopes they will find an opportunity to cut their teeth while they're with the wagon train. He wants them to return to the village as warriors."

Trent shook his head. "That might make them reckless."

One of the young men stopped petting a strawberry roan and put his bridle on the horse. "We are not reckless."

"You speak the white man's tongue. How is that?" Trent asked.

"We trade. We travel much to trade. I go with Two Moons when he traded. I learned words of white man traders," the man said as he finished bridling the horse and vaulted onto his back.

"What's your name?" Pat asked.

"Boy Without Pony," the man replied.

"That's a little long. We'll just call you Pony Boy," Trent said as he watched the war chief and his companion ride away.

"Do you know how to shoot the pistol you're packing?" Wes asked.

"Yes. I learned when very small. Father taught me. He said bows were old way. We must use the white man's tools."

Wes nodded. "Smart man, your father. Was he with the other Arapahos earlier?"

Pony Boy shook his head. "No. Father die at Sand Creek."

Wes exchanged glances with Trent and Pat.

"Pony Boy, tell the other men to ride their horses across the river ahead of the first wagon. We need to see where the deep spots are located," Pat said.

Pony Boy quickly turned to his companions and ordered them to mount and follow him across the river.

One Arapaho man, bigger than the others, objected to Pony Boy giving orders. Pat realized what was happening and walked Leo over to the big man as he mounted his horse. Pat made abrupt signs with both hands and pointed in the direction the war chief had taken.

The man bowed his head as he made returns signs. Then he followed the rest of the Arapahos as they rode in front of the lead wagon and waded their horses into the swiftly moving water.

"What was that all about, Pat?" Wes asked.

"The big man didn't want to take orders from Pony Boy. I told him I had appointed Pony Boy chief of the group. And if he didn't want to follow his orders, he could return to his camp," Pat said.

"He didn't seem to want to return to his people," Wes said.

Pat nodded. "He would have brought great shame upon himself if he had returned."

"Look," Trent called out as he urged Tex to the edge of the riverbank. "One of the men is in trouble."

A horse had stumbled as it stepped into a hole and fell forward, tossing its rider into the water. The horse regained his footing, but the current had caught the man and pulled him downstream.

Trent uncoiled his lasso as he paralleled the man's movement downstream. The man spotted Trent and struggled to swim toward the bank. Trent swirled his lariat over his head as the man inched nearer to the bank. Finally, using his knees to guide Tex, Trent directed the horse into the water. As he did so, he cast his lariat. The lasso fell over the man's shoulders. The man quickly grabbed the rope as Trent urged Tex toward the bank. As the man climbed out of the water, he made a sign which Trent took to mean thank you.

"Pat, tell the man he can thank me by not eating my dog," Trent called over to his brother.

"I didn't know you were so good with a lasso," Wes said when Trent rode back to the wagon crossing. "You've got to teach me."

Trent nodded over at Pat, who had retrieved the riderless horse. "Pat's better with a rope than me. He's the one to learn from."

The crossing took hours. Pat and Trent, having seen where the deep holes were in the river, guided each wagon across. The wagon train made several miles after the crossing before they circled the wagons.

Bruce had worried the settlers would have to feed the warriors, but they hunted and bagged enough rabbits for their own meal. Becky joined everyone at the cookfire for the first time since the Comanche attack. The fare was bacon, beans, and biscuits. Trent eyed Becky throughout the meal but didn't attempt to start a conversation.

"Bruce," Trent called out as he finished his last biscuit. "The Arapaho men might come in handy should we need to find an alternate source of water."

"Well, I guess if we run into trouble with dry water holes, the Arapahos might earn their twenty horses," Bruce said.

"Trent," Pat called out. "Pony Boy reminds me of us. His father was a trader, the same as ours."

"Yeah," Wes said. "He reminds me of you, Pat. You two could be cousins."

"Yup, white man say all Indians look alike," Pat said.

"Dang it, Pat. I never know when you're serious or teasing. Your face never changes," Wes declared.

Becky got up off the barrel she had been sitting on and walked over to where her mother was cleaning the metal plates.

Lois shook her off. "Becky, you go and rest. I can clean up by myself."

Wes glanced over at Trent. "Sis ain't back to normal yet."

Trent nodded. "Yup, I know."

"She's getting better every day," Lois said. "She doesn't sleep all day like she did after we left Fort Dodge."

Trent sighed. "Let's hope she returns to her old self."

*No No— needs to be a much better/nicer person — not her old self — She'll cause problems with the Indians —*

# Chapter Eight
# Pony Boy

Bruce motioned for Trent to follow him after they finished their morning vittles. He waited until he was out of hearing range of Becky. "We're out of water."

Trent motioned to Pony Boy, who had just ridden up to the Cowans' wagon. The young, wiry man reined his horse over to them. "When will we reach the water hole? The settlers are running out of water."

Pony Boy pointed his finger skyward. "Today, when the sun is at high point in sky."

"We have to work on his English," Bruce said.

"English?" Pony Boy repeated the word.

"White man tongue," Trent said.

"Called English?"

Trent nodded, "Yup."

"Have one of your men ride ahead to see if there's water," Trent said.

"I ride."

"No, you are the only one who speaks the white man's tongue..."

"English!" Pony Boy said proudly.

"Yup, English. So send another man," Trent ordered.

Pony Boy made a hand sign that meant okay and turned his horse around and rode back the way he had come.

"He's a likable chap," Bruce said. "And I see him hanging out with Pat and Wes."

"Yup, they are teaching him how to draw his old Colt Dragoon."

Bruce shook his head. "They're teaching him to be a quick draw artist. I'm thinking that might be a bad idea. He's probably gotten his mind set on killing soldiers for revenge of the Sand Creek massacre. He said his father died there."

Trent shrugged. "The bluecoats will get their comeuppance, I guess."

"Hmm, it's easy to forget you're half Yaqui."

"When treaties are broken, it's usually the white man who breaks them," Trent reminded Bruce.

"Yeah, I guess you're right. But there's got to be space for the settlers. Anyway... let's get the wagons moving. The sooner we get to the watering hole, the sooner the oxen can drink."

Trent gave a nod. "I'll go see if Pony Boy has sent one of the men ahead to the water hole."

Trent found the young men still gathered around their campfire. They all gave Trent their full attention when he rode up. Only Pony Boy gave him the palm up greeting.

The big man who had bucked when Pat told him he had to take orders from Pony Boy stared at Trent as a dog stares at a cat. Trent had learned from Pat that the man's name was One Moon and he was the son of the war chief, Two Moons. Trent could see why the man objected to taking orders from Pony Boy.

"Did you send someone to scout out the water hole?" Trent asked.

"I sent Runs With Deer. He has a fast horse. He back soon."

"Good. Let me know as soon as he returns," Trent said before reining Tex around and heading back to the Cowans' wagon. The sight of Becky sitting on the seat beside her mother brought a smile to Trent's face as he pulled alongside the wagon.

He tipped his hat. "Morning, Becky." He didn't expect an answer.

"I'm tired of riding in the wagon. I want to ride my horse," Becky said. _Snot_ —

"Oh, really? I'll fetch the saddle and get her ready," Trent said in a cheery tone as he slipped off Tex and walked the horse to the back of the wagon where Becky's Morgan mare was tied. Having saddled her horse numerous times, Trent knew where to find her tack just inside the back tailgate of the wagon.

Wes must have seen Trent saddling Becky's horse because he rode up. "Well, you couldn't be smiling bigger if you had just eaten a piece of apple pie."

"Don't you have work to do, like giving Pony Boy gunslinger lessons?" Trent replied as he tightened the cinches.

"Nah, that's Pat's job. Mine is teaching him English."

"On that you are failing something awful."

"Well, I ain't no teacher. What do you expect?"

Trent nodded. "About what I'm hearing."

"Now feel free to step in and do a better job," Wes said.

"Nah, I've got more important things to."

"You best be teasing!" Wes said.

Trent laughed. "Gee, it's so easy to get your bristles up, Wes. You let a gunslinger get under your skin, and you'll be visiting boot hill."

Wes shook his head. "Goodness, I hope I don't have to live with you as a brother-in-law."

Trent's expression turned sober. "Well, now, a while back, I would have bet the pot I would be joining the family. Now, I think it's going to be a long ride for it to happen."

"We'll see," Wes said as he wheeled Major around. "I'll go and jaw with Pony Boy and see if I can stop him from sounding offensive to your ears."

"What were you and Wes talking about?" Becky said as Trent matched pace with the wagon while leading Tex and Lady.

"Teaching Pony Boy how to speak the white man's tongue," Trent said. "Here, let me help you down so Bruce doesn't have to stop the wagon."

"Thanks," Becky said once her feet touched the ground. She took the reins of the mare. "I just want to ride alongside the wagon. You don't have to stay."

"Oh, I thought you wanted to take a real ride," Trent said and sounded disappointed. *WOW!*

"Another day, maybe. Now run along. I'm sure you have chores to do," Becky said in a dismissive tone.

Trent wheeled Tex abruptly around and rode ahead of the wagon. He let Tex have his bit and galloped the big stallion for a mile up the trail. He pulled Tex to a sudden stop when he spotted a rider riding like the devil was on his tail.

*Back to the old old Boston Becky!*

Shading his eyes, Trent realized it was Runs With Deer, sent to scout out the water hole. "Well, now, Tex, this can't be good."

Hearing horse hooves behind him, Trent turned in the saddle. Pony Boy had spotted the man, too. He arrived at Trent's side before the rider reached them.

Immediately, Runs With Deer started speaking and accompanied his words with hand gestures. Pony Boy waited until the man finished his report before he turned to Trent.

"Water hole is poisoned. Drink water, get sick and die. Four settlers dead at water hole. Drink water, you die," Pony Boy said.

Trent took his hat off and banged it against his leg. "Dang it! We're out of water. If we don't get fresh water, the oxen will all die. Then the settlers!" He shook his head violently. "Come on, let's tell Bruce." Trent wore a grim expression when the three of them reached the Cowans' wagon.

"Lord help us if the news is as bad as your expression," Bruce said the moment he saw Trent's face.

"The water is poisoned. Probably arsenic! From what the scout said."

Bruce stopped the team of oxen. "We need water. We don't have enough for the oxen. They won't make it another day."

Trent turned to Pony Boy. "Is there another water hole we can reach before nightfall?"

Pony Boy, instead of answering, glanced at the man who had scouted the water hole. He said something to him. Runs With Deer reacted angrily, as though Pony Boy had told him something insulting.

Don't they wonder who poisoned the water hole?

"What's going on, Pony Boy?" Trent asked.

"There safe water hole nearby. It on sacred ground. White men are forbidden to enter," Pony Boy said.

Bruce took a step toward Pony Boy's horse. "But our oxen will all die without water."

Suddenly, Runs With Deer whipped his horse around and galloped toward the rear of the wagon train where the other Arapaho were scattered alongside the wagons.

Trent glanced at Pony Boy. "Where is he heading?"

"He tells One Moon."

"Do you have to have One Moon's permission to take us to the water hole?" Trent asked.

"He leader, not me. I tell the others what you want them to do. The decision not mine," Pony Boy said.

"Dang it," Bruce swore. "We agreed to bring them along in case we needed them to show us alternative water holes."

The sound of horses caused Bruce and Trent to glance back along the line of wagons. The entire group of Arapaho approached. Lobo didn't seem to like them converging on their location and let out a low growl.

"What's going on?" Pat said as he and Wes rode up.

"The water hole is poisoned. The Arapaho know of another one nearby, but it's on sacred ground. I think Pony Boy wants to take us there, but he can't make that decision. One Moon has the authority, not him."

Pat shook his head. "One Moon hates Pony Boy and the settlers. He's not going to let us set foot on sacred ground."

Pony Boy, who had been listening, nodded his head. "Pat right. One Moon say no."

"But can't Pony Boy show us the way?" Bruce said with a hint of desperation in his voice.

Pat shook his head. "He can't. Only a chief can permit us to enter sacred grounds."

"That's that! There's no chief among the men. Dang it, they aren't even full-fledged warriors," Bruce called out angrily.

If looks could kill, the one that One Moon gave Pony Boy would have sent him to boot hill. One Moon started speaking as soon as he stopped his horse in front of Pony Boy. He spoke in a loud tone, and used abrupt hand signals to add emphasis to his words.

"He's telling Pony Boy he is a disgrace to the Arapaho. That he should fall upon his knife in shame at mentioning the sacred place to the white men."

Pony Boy paused for a long moment before he answered. Pat shook his head as he listened. Even before Pony Boy finished speaking, One Moon moved his rifle from the crook of his arm and started to point it at Pony Boy. However, the butt of the Winchester did not reach One Moon's shoulder. Pony Boy drew his pistol with the speed of a striking rattler. He shot One Moon in the chest. *oh No —*

The young warriors watched in shock as their leader slipped off his horse. One Moon struck the ground face first and didn't move. Lobo ran up and sniffed One Moon, then turned and walked back to stand beside Tex.

Pat drew his pistols and pointed them at the men. "Pony Boy, tell them to take One Moon and return to their camp. Tell them I will kill anyone who makes a threatening move."

Pony Boy quickly relayed the message. Trent leveled his Sharps at the group, and Wes drew his pistol to back up Pony Boy's words. One of the men urged his horse forward a step. He rapidly fired angry words at Pony Boy. When he finished, he signaled two of his companions to load One Moon on his horse. Once they had laid One Moon across his horse, he took up the reins. Before he turned to leave, he made an abrupt sign at Pony Boy.

"What was all that about?" Bruce asked.

Trent shrugged.

"It was the sign of a ghost. From now on, Pony Boy is invisible to the Arapaho," Pat said.

Trent glanced at Pony Boy. The young Arapaho's face looked ashen. "Pony Boy, you are not a ghost. We see you. You are one with us!"

"Yes," Bruce said. "We are your people now."

"When I die, my spirit bound to the earth. I no hunt in the afterlife," Pony Boy said.

"Live for now, Pony Boy. Don't worry about tomorrow," Wes said. "If you want to hunt, do it now!"

"Pony Boy," Bruce said with desperation. "Will you lead us to the water hole?" *Oh no —*

"Yes. I lead you," he said.

"Which way?" Bruce asked eagerly.

Pony Boy pointed to a big outcropping of huge multicolored boulders. "It is among the painted rocks."

"Lordy me!" Bruce exclaimed. "That's only an hour away."

"Let's ride ahead and scout it out," Pat told Pony Boy. "Wes, you ride with us."

"What made him turn against his people?" Becky, who had to watch the entire proceedings, called from her saddle.

Trent shrugged as he frowned. "I guess the white man's world had more attraction than the Arapaho's. That and the fact he made friends with Pat and Wes. They act like they are three brothers."

"Let's hope the water is there, and it's good," Bruce said. He sighed. "I'm going to put my faith in Pony Boy, Trent. Let's head the wagons for the painted rocks."

"Yup, I'm sure there's water," Trent said. He glanced at Becky and tipped his hat. "Maybe you'll take a real ride tomorrow, Becky."

Becky nodded. "Maybe, Trent. Maybe."

# Chapter Nine
# The Desert

"How many days to the Canadian River?" Bruce asked as he adjusted his bandanna over his nose to keep the dust out of his nose.

"We'll reach it by nightfall if we don't stop," Trent said. "But if we stop in this dust storm, we're going to lose some oxen. At the river, we can keep their noses washed clean of dust."

"Why oxen? What makes the dust worst for them than the horses?"

Trent leaned closer to the wagon to shelter from the windblown dust. "It's their nose. If the dust clogs up their nose, they will overheat and die."

"Really? I didn't know that. Is there anything we can do?"

"Maybe. I'm thinking we can tie bandannas over their nose and switch them when they get clogged. It works for us. It might work for the oxen," Trent said.

"Then ride around and tell the wagons to do it. I guess if they don't have enough bandannas, they can cut up bedsheets and use them," Bruce said.

Trent nodded and immediately led Tex away from the wagon and mounted. The blowing sand cut visibility to the length of two wagons. He had already warned the settlers to keep as close to the wagon they were following as possible. Some had even tied ropes from the yoke of their lead oxen to the tailgate of the wagon ahead of them. Pat, Wes, and Pony stood nearby, waiting for Trent.

"What are we going to do?" Wes asked.

Trent explained what he had discussed with Bruce.

"It might work," Pat said. "But they must change the bandannas if they get covered with dust, or the beasts won't be able to breathe."

"Yup, now let's visit every wagon and tell the settlers what they must do. Some aren't going to like ripping up their bedsheets. Tell them it's better to lose a few bedsheets than their wagons. Wes, you start from the rear and work toward the front. Pat, you start in the middle and work toward the rear. I'll start here and work back."

"Okay," Pat called out above the howling of the wind.

"All right, Lobo, it's just you and me. Let's get to work," Trent said as he rode back to the wagon trailing the Cowans'. Dan Murphy waved to him as he approached the man walking beside his team of oxen. Lobo walked up and sniffed the man's leg.

"He ain't going to bite, is he?" Dan asked.

Trent shook his head. "Not unless you smell like a biscuit."

"As my wife tells it, I smell worse than a polecat," Dan said. "I wonder if this sand bath I'm getting will improve my odor?"

After Trent stopped chuckling, he told Dan what he should do to his oxen and then rode back to the next wagon.

John Cooper, a tall man with a full Lincoln beard, waved his whip at Trent as he approached. "When is this dadburn storm going to pass?" he shouted.

"Sometimes they last for days. There's no telling when it will end."

Suddenly John glanced around. "Where is Jethro? He was walking beside me a moment ago!"

The image of a towheaded boy of ten flashed through Trent's mind as John called out the boy's name. The howling wind killed the reach of his voice. John's wife, on the other side of the oxen, shouted to him, wanting to know why he was calling Jethro's name. John yelled that Jethro was missing and for her to stay where she was.

After a while, John stopped yelling the boy's name and turned to Trent. "The oxen were having trouble pulling the load, so I tossed out some furniture and made Jethro walk on this side of the wagon with me. Dora is on the other side with Judy."

"You can't stop the wagon. We have to keep moving. I'll go and look for the boy," Trent said. "He couldn't have wandered far."

"Mr. Trent, you got to find my boy. He's my life," John shouted to be heard over the wind.

"I will," Trent said as he reined Tex around. "Come on, Lobo. We've got to find the boy." Trent decided to ride about twenty yards from the wagon and headed back toward the rear of the wagon train. He figured the boy had veered off to the right and got lost. He didn't know if the boy would keep walking away from the wagon or try to turn around and head back.

However, there was no way the boy could tell directions in the low visibility. Trent even found it difficult to know which way he was heading. Only by looking up and trying to figure out the brightest spot in the sandstorm could he figure out where the sun stood in the sky.

About twenty minutes later, he still hadn't seen hide nor hair of the boy. He rode back in sight of one of the wagons. He felt it was hopeless looking for the boy in the storm. However, he couldn't bring himself to give up.

"Come on Lobo, let's head back out and search some more." This time, he rode about fifty yards to the right of the wagons and headed up the trail. Shouting the boy's name as he rode, Trent kept looking right and left. Nothing.

It was hopeless! Even the entire wagon train couldn't locate the boy in the storm. And if they stopped, they would lose oxen and maybe other settlers to the storm. No, Trent decided, he couldn't stop the wagon train to look for the boy. Having made that decision, he turned Tex back toward the wagons.

Once he caught up to the wagon train, he headed toward the front. He dreaded facing John Cooper with the bad news. The man was sure to take losing the boy to heart. Mr. Cooper spotted Trent the moment he appeared out of the blowing sand.

"Where's my boy? Where is Jethro? Lord, where is my boy?"

Trent shook his head. "Sorry. I tried. The visibility is too bad. I couldn't find him. There's no use searching in the storm."

"We must stop and search for him!" Dora screamed as she ran around the oxen team to confront Trent.

Trent shook his head. "We can't. We have to keep moving or we lose the oxen."

"Darn the oxen!" John shouted. "My boy's life is worth more than all my oxen!"

"John, if we lose the oxen, we lose the wagons. Lose enough wagons and settlers are going to die, maybe your wife and daughter among them. We have to keep pushing through the storm until we reach the Canadian River! We'll reach it tonight. Once the storm peters out, I'll take Pat, Wes, and Pony Boy and search for him.

"He will be dead by then!" John yelled.

"Not if he hunkers down. He can survive."

John shook his head. "No, I'm stopping!"

Trent shifted his Sharps and pointed it at the settler. "No, you're going to keep moving. I'm not going to lose you and the rest of your family. If you stop, your oxen will die. You'll have nothing, no oxen, no wagon, and no supplies."

"Papa," Judy, a girl of about eight years old, called out as she lifted the bandana from her face. She wiped muddy tears from her cheeks with the back of her hand. "Can I get back into the wagon? The sand is burning my eyes."

"Yes, baby," Dora spoke up before John. "Come along. I'll put you in the wagon."

"Come on, John, you got to keep the oxen walking," Trent shouted. "Get moving! The wagon behind you is closing in on yours."

"You can go to blazes, Trent. Shoot me if you will, but I'm stopping and going to look for my son."

Suddenly, a piercing scream cut through the roar of the wind. Trent and John glanced at the wagon. Dora stood behind the seat, cradling Jethro in her arms.

"What?" John shouted as he ran back to the wagon. "Where did you find him?"

"Asleep in the back of the wagon," his wife called out as tears ran down her cheeks.

"Pa, I got tired of walking. Are you mad at me for getting in the wagon?"

"I should be. I should whip you good," John said as he reached up and ran his fingers through the boy's long blond hair.

"John," Trent called out. "Get your wagon moving!"

"Trent, you are a curly wolf if I ever met one. We are not friends. I'm leaving this wagon train the first chance I get," John said.

"That's fine and dandy, Mr. Cooper, but until that time, you will take orders. Now put some bandannas over the noses of your oxen and get your team moving!" Trent glanced down at Lobo. "Come on, we still have the others to warn."

A little later, Trent met Pat, Wes, and Pony Boy headed back to the Cowans' wagon.

"Trent, we've been looking for you. Where did you get off to?" Wes asked.

"I went on a wild goose chase trying to find a boy in the storm, only for his sister to find him asleep in the wagon," Trent said.

"I'm surprised you didn't get lost in the storm," Wes said. "You can't see more than a wagon length ahead of yourself."

"You forget, I'm half Yaqui," Trent said.

An hour before the lead wagon reached the Canadian River, the wind died down as quickly as it had sprung up. It pleased Trent that they hadn't lost a single animal. He had heard of similar sandstorms taking a terrible toll among the oxen teams.

"Dang it, brother," Pat said. "For a while there, I didn't think we were all going to make it. That idea of yours to cover the oxen's noses with the bandannas worked wonders."

"The moment we get the wagons circled, I'm going to take a bath in the river," Trent said. "I feel like I'm carrying enough dirt to plant corn."

"Why don't you and the boys ride up and check out the crossing? I hope no one's waiting for us like at the Cimarron." As usual, no expression betrayed Pat's inner thoughts.

Trent smiled. "Come on, Pat. Bring your friends," Trent said as he trotted Tex toward the line of pine and cottonwood trees that signaled the river.

"Once we cross the Canadian, we're on our last leg of the trail to Santa Fe," Pat said.

"What happens after Santa Fe?" Wes asked.

Trent shrugged. "Some wagons will peel off and head south. Others will continue to California."

"Becky and Ma want to continue to California," Wes said. "But Pa will start looking for a place to homestead. Pat, Pony Boy, and I are thinking about continuing on west, maybe not all the way to California. We are thinking about signing on with a cattle drive."

Trent glanced at Pat. "Playing cowboy?"

"There are worse things," Pat said.

Pony Boy just grinned.

Trent shook his head. "Lord, help the trail boss with you three in the saddle."

Pat pointed toward a low point in the riverbank as they neared the Canadian River. "There's the crossing. The bank of the river is too steep elsewhere for the wagons to cross."

"Let's hope this is going to be easier than the last one," Trent said as they approached the riverbank.

"Trent," Pat called out. "What's that on the other side of the river, along the bank?"

"Dadburn it. It's a fence. Some galoot strung up wire!" Trent proclaimed.

"Those white men!" Pony Boy nodded his head to several men resting in the shade of a big ponderosa pine.

Wes shook his head. "So much for an easy crossing."

"Go get your pa," Trent said as he shifted his Sharps as though itching to use it.

How much to cross?

# Chapter Ten
# Don't Fence Me In

Bruce stared across the river at the eight men holding rifles. "I thought the Santa Fe Trail was government land."

Trent nodded. "Yeah, well, someone staked a homestead claim on this section." He pointed to a small pine log shack. "There's their home, sorry sight that it is."

"What do we do?" Bruce asked.

"You two go over and see what they want in payment for us to cross. I guess if it's not much, we should pay it and avoid a fight."

"And if they want too much?" Bruce asked.

Trent shrugged. "We kill them."

"But that would make us murderers!" Bruce protested.

"Not if what they are doing is illegal." Pat spoke up. "You can only homestead sections of land the government opens to homesteading. And I'm sure this isn't one of those sections."

"You are just full of learning," Wes said.

Trent shook his head. "Take Wes, Pat, and Pony Boy with you, Bruce. I'll cover y'all from here," he said as he dismounted. "Anyone looks as they are going to open fire I'll put in the dirt."

"I sure hope it doesn't come down to that," Bruce said as he urged his horse toward the river.

Wes, Pat, and Pony Boy followed him into the river.

Trent propped his rifle on a rock as he took a seated firing position. He lined the sights up on the man who walked forward to wait from them at the riverbank.

The man blocked them from riding onto the bank. Trent could hear Bruce's voice as he greeted the man, but he couldn't follow the conversation. The longer the conversation continued, the louder the voices grew. Then the man facing them made the mistake of bringing his Winchester up to threaten Bruce.

Trent squeezed the trigger.

Even before the loud rifle shot died, the Winchester dropped from the man's grip and he grabbed his upper arm with his left hand. Trent swung his sights to cover the men behind the leader. He fired again as another man raised his rifle, only to get nicked in the arm and drop it.

Pat called out something as he drew his pistols. Then Wes and Pony Boy reached for their irons. Bruce yelled something. Wes and Pony Boy holstered their guns, but Pat continued to cover the group of men as they dropped their rifles.

Figuring it was time he joined them, Trent mounted Tex and guided him into the river.

"A couple of you men get over here and help your boss," Bruce said as Tex climbed onto the bank.

"You can't just ride through my homestead," the leader said as one of his men ripped the sleeve of his shirt to look at the wound.

Cory - Leader
Buck

"It ain't too bad," the man said after he examined the arm.

"I could just as easily have put you in the dirt," Trent said as he urged Tex toward the wounded man.

"I'll report y'all to the marshal in Wagon Mound for trespassing."

Trent shook his head. "Nah, you won't. You know what you're doing is illegal. We're going to burn your shack down, and you and your gang are going to hightail it someplace where we ain't."

"Cory, we've been bested," one of his men called out.

"Yeah," the man tending Cory's arm agreed. "I told you we were going to come up against a wagon train that would brace us."

"Shut your pie hole, Buck, and bandage my arm."

Trent nodded over at the men. "Pull your pistols out and drop them. Pat will shoot anyone who tries something funny. After you disarm, you'll gather your belongings from the shack and get on your horses. And head for the hills!" He watched as the men tossed their pistols onto the ground. "Wes will gather your guns and return them to you when you're mounted, ready to ride."

"You dang sure haven't seen the last of me," Cory said as he shrugged Buck's hands off him and walked toward the shack.

Trent ignored Cory. "Pat, you and Pony Boy go with them and keep them from doing something foolish while they're gathering their belongings."

Once they were alone, Trent turned to Bruce. "What did they demand for tribute?"

"Five dollars a wagon. If it had been just a dollar, I would have paid it."

Trent shook his head. "Nah, it's best this way. We're saving some smaller wagon trains grief at the hands of the gang."

"Yeah, I guess you're right," Bruce said. "So this is the Canadian River?"

"Yup."

"It flows down through the panhandle of Texas, don't it?" Bruce asked.

"Yup, why ask?"

"I've been jawing with Lois about settling in Texas instead of continuing on to California. She's agreed."

"What about Becky? I thought she wanted to keep on to California." *She's got No Say — She's a kid — see!*

Bruce shook his head. "She ain't got a say in this. Later, if she's a mind to go on to California, I can't stop her. But that time ain't now."

*DiDn't Answer →* "What about the wagon train? You're the wagon master," Trent said.

"I'll continue as far as Wagon Mound with the wagons. Then I'm going to leave them. I'll get supplies I need to build a cabin, maybe some livestock, and return here. I plan on following the Canadian River until I find a spot to homestead." Bruce paused. "What about you? Are you continuing with the wagon train?"

Trent shook his head. "No, Bruce, if it is okay with you, I'll see you to the end and help you with building your cabin. One man can't build a log cabin by himself."

"I'll have Wes." *MAybe —*

Trent shook his head. "Don't be too sure of that. He, Pat, and Pony Boy keep talking about continuing west."

"I'm surprised the two have taken to Pony Boy so much," Bruce said.

"They're kindred spirits."

"I guess you're right."

"Even if they intend to continue west, I'll get Pat to stick around and help with the homestead."

"Why not homestead a section next to me?" Bruce asked.

"Let's see what happens."

"Okay. I guess I better be getting back to the wagons and get them ready for the crossing," Bruce said as he turned his horse toward the river.

"I'll be along shortly. I just want to make sure nothing goes sideways here."

Later, as Trent, Pat, Wes, and Pony Boy crossed the river, Trent nodded at Wes. "Did you know your pa is leaving the wagon train at Wagon Mound?"

"Yeah, I heard," Wes said.

"Are you going with him?" Trent asked.

"Are you?" Wes tossed the question back at Trent.

"Yup. I figured I would at least stick around until he gets his cabin up."

Wes nodded over at Pat and Pony Boy. "I discussed it with those two. We decided to help him with setting up the homestead. After that, we are all heading west."

"Good, he's going to need all the help he can get," Trent said as they approached the lead wagon.

"Fellows, is it going to be an easy crossing?" a woman wearing a blue bonnet asked as she walked beside her oxen.

"I hope so, Mrs. Creel," Trent called out to her as they rode past.

They found Bruce walking beside his oxen with Lois on the other side. Becky sat in the wagon seat.

"Pa told me you didn't kill anyone, Trent."

Trent nodded. "That's right, I just winged a couple of galoots."

"Good, I don't like all this killing," Becky said.

"Trent," Bruce said as he rode up. "You all go up and escort the wagons across the river. When I crossed, I didn't find any holes, just some rocks. I think the wagons will make it across without any problems, at least I hope so."

"Sure, Bruce," Trent replied. He glanced at Becky. "After we cross, would you like to go for a ride along the river?"

Becky smiled. "Yeah, I think I would like that."

"Good," Trent said before he turned Tex around. "Come on, boys, let's see that the wagons get across safely."

Wes spurred his Quarter Horse, and the race to the river was on. Wes's horse sprinted ahead, but Pat's mustang caught the Quarter Horse at the halfway mark and passed him. Pony Boy's horse couldn't match the other three's speed and finished last. Trent didn't mind coming in third, as he knew Tex could outrun the other three mounts in a longer race.

Once the wagons started to cross the river, Trent and Wes stayed on the right side of the wagons while Pat and Pony Boy watched the wagons from the other bank. Lobo paced back and forth at the edge of the river while he stared at Trent.

Trent figured as long as the wagons stayed between them, they wouldn't run into any trouble. He kept yelling at the drovers to keep the oxen directly behind the wagon in front of them. However, Bill Bennett let his oxen stray to the right. He drove the oxen alone. His wife sat in the wagon seat. She had an infant in her arms and had to oversee four boys ranging in age from three to seven.

"Get back into position, Bill!" Trent shouted as the wagon passed him.

He spotted the youngest boy standing against the tailgate of the wagon. He started to call out to his mother to fetch the boy when the wagon wheel hit a rock and caused the wagon to bounce. In horror, Trent saw the boy fall over the tailgate and into the river. Even as he urged Tex toward the spot where the child had fallen, he spotted the boy's head bobbing up and down as the current took him downstream.

The mother screamed, and Bill glanced back. "Little Walter fell out of the wagon," his wife shouted.

"I'm after him," Trent shouted as he rode between the wagons.

Pat and Pony Boy hadn't seen the boy fall into the water. They tried to see what was causing all the commotion. Pat spotted Trent wading downriver and realized someone must have fallen. He rushed to follow Trent.

The rocky river bottom made the going slow for Tex. He couldn't keep pace with the speed of the current. Seeing the bobbing head of the boy getting farther away, Trent reined Tex toward the bank. Once on dry land, he raced downriver. He caught sight of the boy, only to lose him as the current pulled him under.

Realizing he had to get ahead of the boy, Trent galloped Tex forty yards ahead of the boy and dismounted. As Lobo barked at him, Trent shucked his gun belt and kicked off his boots before plunging into the river. He swam as hard as he could and managed to get in the middle of the river. He dug his toes into the rocks and fought the current as he waited for the bouncing head of the boy to drift within reach.

When the current brought the boy near him, Trent lunged for him and grabbed him round the neck. He lifted the boy's head out of the water as he fought his way toward the shore.

Pat waited for him. He took the boy from his brother and laid him on his back and pressed the palm of his hand against the boy's belly. Water squirted out of the boy's mouth. Pat repeated the action, and more water ran out of the boy's mouth.

"Come on kid, breathe!" Trent mumbled.

Suddenly, the boy coughed up more water. Lobo ran up and licked the boy in the face and frightened him. The boy started to cry. It was a beautiful sound to Trent's ears.

He walked over and glanced down at the boy. "Pat, I thought he was a goner for sure."

Pat looked up at his brother. "Trent, you dragged him out of the water just in time." He lifted the boy. "I'll take him back to his wagon while you dry out a bit."

Trent glanced over at Lobo. "Yup, you come running up at the end and try to take credit for saving the boy. Well, you didn't do nothing but bark, nothing but bark."

# Chapter Eleven
# It Ain't Over

"I hate burning a cabin when I'm going to have to build one," Bruce said as he watched the fake settlers' shack burn.

Trent shook his head. "If we didn't burn it, they would just return after we leave and prey on the next wagon train."

"Yeah, I reckon you're right, but I still hate burning it." Bruce wiped the sweat off his forehead with his bandanna. "Trent, I swear, if I had known we would face such dangers on the Santa Fe Trail, I would never have moved west."

Trent smiled. "I'm glad you did, Bruce, or I would never have met your daughter. *you would have been better off — I never have liked her —*

"I see things are back on the right path between you *especially* two." *in book 1 — maybe she be better in book 3 —*

Trent nodded. "They're moseying along that way. Which reminds me, I told Becky I would take her for a ride."

"Where you and Becky off to?"

"I thought to ride down the river a way."

"Yeah, well, I'm hoping that after Wagon Mound, we can follow the Canadian into Texas. I'm eager to get settled."

"Yup, the idea of claiming a homestead has been rattling round in my head lately," Trent admitted. "Well, I better go and saddle Becky's mare."

"Yeah, you go ahead. The wagons are all circled. There's nothing to do until Lois calls us for vittles."

Things had finally turned around between Trent and Becky. For a while, he didn't think their relationship would get back on track. Trent whistled as he saddled the mare.

"Hmm, I know why you're whistling," Wes said as he stopped his Quarter Horse behind the wagon. "It's Sis. She's stopped giving you the cold shoulder."

Trent glanced at Wes and smiled.

"I told you she would come around. She can't resist your blue eyes. She told me that once."

"Ah, Wes, you're just making that up. But I like it anyway. Now run along and finish making your rounds." After Wes left, Trent quickly finished saddling the mare and walked both horses around to the front of the wagon.

"I heard every word you and Wes said," Becky declared. "Shame on y'all for talking behind my back."

Trent blushed. "Here, let me help you off the wagon," Trent said, ignoring Becky as she laughed at his expense.

"Is the smoke from the outlaws' shack?" Becky asked as she mounted. "It's a shame we had to burn it."

"Yup, that was your pa's sentiments," Trent said as he mounted Tex. "I figured we would ride down the river a way. Keep in the shade of the ponderosas."

"Good, I enjoy the smell of pine needles."

They didn't speak again until they reached the bank of the river. "Are you still set on going to California?" Trent asked.

"No, I've had enough of the trail. I want to stay in one place. I'm just hoping that Pa finds a place to settle near a town. I don't want to be stuck in the cabin for months without seeing another soul."

"Becky, I've been batting around the idea of putting down roots. I'm thinking of staking out a claim to a nice piece of land along the Canadian, too."

"You aren't going to keep heading west? Wes said he and Pat and Pony Boy were heading to Arizona after they helped Pa with the log cabin."

"No, I'm tired of sleeping in the open and staying in the saddle all day. I've never really had a permanent home. My father was a trader. We moved around in a wagon," Trent said as they approached some boulders not far from the riverbank. A big pine grew near the rocks. He was thinking about stopping and resting in the shade.

"I've decided one of those fancy California gentlemen couldn't have saved me from that Comanche, Trent. And you saving that little boy. That makes you a hero in my eyes."

"Becky, do you want to stop and rest in the shade near those rocks?" Trent found the courage to ask.

Becky urged her mare toward the rocks and the big pine. "That would be nice."

Lobo, who had been walking beside Tex, suddenly growled and disappeared. The sound of a gun cocking startled Becky. Trent shifted his Sharps to his shoulder.

"Drop the rifle, or I shoot the calico," called out a voice.

Trent immediately recognized it as belonging to Cory, the man who had demanded payment for the wagon train to cross the river.

"Drop it, I tell you!" Cory yelled as he rode out from behind the rocks with a pistol in his left hand. His men emerged from both sides of the rocks. "She's kind of pretty to shoot, but I will if you don't drop your rifle and pistol."

"Okay," Trent said. "But I ain't dropping my guns in the dirt. I'll freely give them up, but I'll never drop them on the ground for any man."

"Ah, we have someone here who values his guns over all else. Hey, lady, did you hear that? I threaten to shoot you, and your beau refuses to drop his guns."

Becky spat in Cory's direction.

"Whoa, boys, we have us here a wild cat," Cory said.

"A pretty one at that, boss," one of the riders said.

"Joey and Mick, go over and collect his rifle and pistol while we cover you," Cory ordered. "I told you I wasn't finished with you. I guess you didn't believe me. Now I'm going to take your woman. To get her back, you'll have to pay us five hundred dollars," Cory added as his two men approached Tex.

Tex took a step back.

"Hold him still, mister, or dang it if I won't shoot your nag," the one called Joey said as he rode his buckskin gelding toward Tex.

"Cory, you and your men best turn tail and ride away while you can," Trent said.

"Wow, you have some sand threatening us when we have the drop on you, boy."

Joey reached out his hand. "Hand me the rifle, stock first."

"Lobo!" Trent called out.

A gray streak raced from behind the big ponderosa. Before Cory and his men could get over their surprise, the wolf-dog leaped into the air. His jaws snapped shut on Cory's throat.

As man and dog fell to the ground, Trent swung the butt of his rifle into the side of Joey's head. The man dropped like a rock. Even before Joey's face hit the dirt, Trent drew his pistol. He shot Mick in the head and kept firing his Colt, dropping four more of the riders as quick as he could pull the trigger. Trent held his Sharps out with one arm and blew the last of the riders off the back of his horse.

"Sorry, Becky, if I had dropped my guns, they would have kidnapped you. And dang it, I couldn't let that happen," Trent said.

"Take me back to my wagon, Trent," Becky said, averting her eyes from Lobo, who was still shaking Cory's body.

"Becky, I'm sorry you had to see that," Trent said.

"Please, just take me to the wagon."

"Yeah, sure," Trent said as he grabbed her mare's bridle and turned the horse around. "Come on. Just follow me," he added. He didn't call out to Lobo. He figured the dog deserved to have a little fun.

Pat, Wes, and Pony Boy rode up to meet them a few minutes later.

"What happened? Why all the shots?" Wes yelled as he approached. "Sis! Are you hurt?"

Trent shook his head. "No one got hurt but the bad guys. It was Cory and his boys. They ambushed us and planned to kidnap Becky for ransom."

"Did you kill them all?" Pat asked.

"Yup, well, Lobo killed Cory. Ripped his throat out."

"Sis, are you all right?" Wes asked.

"Take me to the wagon, Wes," Becky said.

"You want me to ride along with you, Becky?" Trent asked.

"No," she answered.

"Okay, you go and relax. I hate you had to see me kill those men," Trent said.

"Please, don't remind me," Becky said as she urged her mare to follow Wes.

"Dang it!" Trent shouted after they left. "Just when things were going so good. I hope Cory is already burning in Hell."

"Where wolf?" Pony Boy asked.

"He ain't finished with his dinner," Trent said. "And we ain't going to bury them. Leave them for crow bait."

"Bruce will probably want to bury them since he plans on returning this way," Pat reminded Trent.

"Well, then he can gather some men. I ain't helping. They don't deserve a decent burial. And I should have killed Cory the first time instead of winging him, and all of this wouldn't have happened!" Trent said.

"You did what you thought was right," Pat said as they headed back to the wagons.

Trent shook his head. "No, I did what I thought Becky would have wanted me to do. I showed mercy. You can't show mercy to outlaws and killers."

"She'll get over it. You saved her from a fate worse than death at the hands of that bunch, I reckon," Pat said.

Bruce waited for them at his wagon. "It never seems to end, Trent. Trouble follows us like a dark cloud."

"No, you've got it wrong, Bruce. We aren't a bunch of bleached bones beside the trail like some settlers. We're alive and healthy. We're the lucky ones."

"I never looked at it that way. And you're right. I keep hearing of settlers who died during Comanche attacks or from bandit raids... and still others from sickness. My entire family is alive and well, and it's because of you and your brother."

"I don't think your daughter sees it that way. She's mighty upset with me for killing those outlaws."

"She's in shock. Once she calms down, she'll realize what would have happened to her had you not put the polecats in the dirt."

"I hope so," Trent said.

"Anyway, y'all come to the cookfire. Lois has biscuits and bacon gravy with some salt pork," Bruce said as he motioned to Pat and Pony Boy to join them.

# Chapter Twelve
# The Cattle Drive

A few days later, Trent turned back in the saddle when he heard a horse approaching. Wes!

"How's it looking up front? No trouble, I hope," Wes said as he stopped beside Trent.

Trent shook his head. "Nope, I haven't seen hide nor hair of an Arapaho except for Pony Boy."

"His English is improving," Wes said.

"How about his pistol lessons?"

"He's mighty fast on the draw. I wouldn't want to brace him."

"That's saying a lot. You think highly of your pistol skills."

"Well, now, I must admit I acknowledge my ability to draw my iron. However, I've come to realize there's always someone quicker."

Trent smiled. "That's an attitude that will keep you alive, Wes. Gunmen who think they can't be beaten, sooner or later, meet their match. Well, except for Pat, of course. He is the fastest."

Wes shook his head. "I ain't going to argue with that, having seen him in action." Wes cleared his throat. "How is it going with Becky? Is she still giving you the cold shoulder?"

he needs a Western woman— not a city snob from Boston!

"It's not cold, but it ain't very warm, either," Trent said. "But she did watch me gun down several men. She has a right to be upset."

Wes shook his head. "No, you killed those outlaws to save her. She should realize that and stop avoiding you."

"Give your sister time. She'll come around. I have faith in her," Trent said. *quit spoiling her —*

Wes pointed. "What's that south of the trail? I hope it's not a dust storm."

Trent shook his head. "Nope. I don't think it's a dust storm."

"Then what?"

Trent squinted. "A big herd of buffalo, maybe. I guess I should ride out and investigate. You go back and tell Bruce and your two friends."

Wes nodded, whipped his Quarter Horse around, and dashed away.

"That boy finds every opportunity to ride hard," Trent mumbled as he urged Tex into a canter. "Come on, Lobo, let's see what's afoot."

Trent hadn't let on to Wes just how much it bothered him that Becky hadn't had much to do with him since the incident along the river. Although he had denied it for a spell, he finally realized Becky had put her brand on him.

Thoughts of Becky vanished as Trent grew closer to the dust cloud. Cattle! A cattle drive, to be specific. Trent had seen cattle drives before, but never a herd the size of the one kicking up the dust cloud. He figured there must be near three thousand head of cattle in the herd.

As he approached, a rider rode out to meet him. "Howdy, pardner," the man said as he stopped his buckskin gelding a few yards from Tex.

"Howdy back to you," Trent said.

The drover nodded at Lobo. "Is that yours?"

"Yup."

"What's your business?" the drover asked, still eying Lobo.

Trent didn't take the man's bluntness as an offense. Drovers had to be careful about strangers. They could be an advance scout for cattle rustlers, or they could do something to spook the herd if they got too close.

"I'm with a wagon train on the Santa Fe Trail. I spotted your dust and rode out to see what caused it."

"Yeah, we're coming up from Texas on the Goodnight-Loving Trail. We're driving the cattle to the railhead in Cheyenne."

Trent shook his head. "You've got a way to go yet. Cheyenne is a distance from our trail."

"I knew we would be crossing the Santa Fe Trail, just didn't realize we were so close."

Trent nodded. "Yup, about two miles north, you'll hit the trail."

"I think McGregor, the owner, will hold the herd on this side of the trail. We can't cross until your wagons are out of the way."

"Yup, we have a long string of ox-drawn wagons. Fifty in all. And at the speed we're both moving, we would block your crossing if you continued. Would be safer to hold the herd back," Trent acknowledged.

"Okay, I'll ride over and tell Mr. McGregor about the wagons," the cowboy said and whipped his horse around and galloped off without another word.

Trent had heard Wes and Pat discussing joining a cattle drive. He didn't think he would like the job of a drover. If you were at the back of the herd, it would be like riding in a dust storm daily. No, he'd already had enough traveling every day and sleeping on the ground. The idea of homesteading along the Canadian River had been growing in his mind over the past few days.

Pat and Pony Boy met Trent about a quarter of a mile from the wagons.

"Buffalo?" Pat asked.

Trent shook his head. "Cattle drive. A huge one, with maybe twenty drovers."

"The way they're heading, the wagons are going to block them from crossing the trail," Pat said.

"Yup, they're going to halt the cattle until we're gone."

"Wes wants to ride with the herd," Pony Boy said. "Be a cowboy."

Trent shook his head. "It's not a life for me. We best ride back and let Bruce know what is going on before he gets excited."

Bruce looked up from his oxen as the four rode up. "What's making all the dust?"

"Cattle drive," Trent replied.

"Must be a big one."

"It is. The drover I met told me they're going to hold up until the wagons get past them," Trent explained.

"Do you think they would sell some steers? We could use fresh meat. I could take up a collection. Maybe buy a couple of head. We could butcher them and have fresh meat for several days."

"Yeah, I'm sure they would. They're heading up the Goodnight-Loving Trail to Cheyenne."

"Hmm, that's a far piece to drive a herd of cattle."

"Pa, it might be fun. Pat, Pony Boy, and I might try our hand at cowboying one of these days," Wes said.

Bruce looked over at Pony Boy. He no longer dressed like an Arapaho. He wore a plaid shirt, dungarees, and a felt hat with a feather in the band. "You want to be a cowboy, Pony Boy?"

"Yes, sir, Mr. Cowan. Pony Boy good rider. I'd make good cowboy, I think."

"I'll take your word for it," Bruce said before he turned his attention back to Trent. "After we circle the wagons, I'll give you what money I collect, and you can go and purchase some steers. We'll take time tomorrow to butcher them before we start out."

"Sounds good, boss," Trent said. He motioned to Pat. "Okay, let's keep the wagons moving. We want to get past the herd as soon as possible." After Pat, Wes, and Pony Boy left, Trent dropped back to the wagon. He tipped his hat at Becky.

"What's making all the dust, Trent?"

"A cattle drive. They're heading to Cheyenne."

"Why drive the cattle so far? Can't they sell them in San Antonio?"

"Yup, but they'll get double the price at the railhead in Cheyenne."

"Well, I don't know anything about cattle drives and don't care to," Becky said.

"Me neither. It's not a job I would take on."

"That's all Wes talks about. That and becoming a bounty hunter. I sure hope he doesn't do that."

"Me too. But Wes and Pat have to make their own decisions," Trent said.

"Are you still pondering settling in Texas with Pa?"

The question caused Trent to smile. "Yup. If'n I find a suitable piece of land."

Becky smiled.

"Well, I better mosey along and try to keep the wagons moving. I'll see you at supper." Trent didn't wait for a reply. He urged Tex into a trot. "Dang it. I ran out of words," he mumbled.

The sun hung low in the west by the time the wagon passed the herd and stopped for the night. Bruce, true to his word, collected money from the wagons and scraped together fifty dollars. He handed the money over to Trent after the wagons had circled.

"What do you think? Can you purchase a couple of steers with fifty dollars?" Bruce asked as he handed the money to Trent.

Trent took the money. "I'll give it a look-see. I'm taking Pat and Pony Boy with me. I'll leave Wes here. I always think it's good to leave at least one person good with a gun with the wagons."

Clint

Bruce nodded. "Yep, with all the bad things that have happened to the wagon train, I agree with you, Trent."

"Okay, cowhands, let's go collect some beef," Trent said with a nod toward Pat and Pony Boy.

The herd had crossed the Santa Fe Trail, and they had been left to graze. As the three approached the chuck wagon, the same rider who had met Trent rode out to greet them.

"Something I can help you gents with?" the cowhand asked. He spoke with an air of authority. Trent figured he must be the trail boss of the cattle drive.

"We were hoping to buy a couple of steers. The settlers need some fresh meat," Trent said.

The clean-shaven cowhand glanced at Pat and Pony Boy disapprovingly for a moment before he nodded. "I reckon you'll have to come and jaw with Mr. McGregor. By the way, my name is Clint."

Trent noted the man had his holster tied to his leg. "I'm Trent." He pointed to Pat. "That's Pat, my brother, and the Arapaho is Pony Boy. Now lead the way, Clint."

The man didn't move. "They aren't going to cause a ruckus, are they?"

"I practice my English," Pony Boy said.

Pat remained silent.

Trent shrugged. "They're tame," he said, knowing that would irk Pat.

Pat broke his silence. "We never cause trouble unless we get trouble."

"I can see you're a salty bunch," the man said. "Well, come along and meet the boss." Since the chuck wagon was on the east side of the herd, Clint had to lead them around milling cattle who were grazing under the watchful eyes of mounted drovers.

"How many cowhands do you have controlling the herd?" Trent asked.

"Twenty-five and four wagons," Clint said as they approached a wagon with its tailgate down and a cookfire behind it. Six men sat around the fire eating from tin plates.

One, a tall, middle-aged, clean-shaven man in a brown duster and Boss of the Plains hat, stood up. He handed his plate to a younger man. Like Trent, the man had broad shoulders, but he had black hair and a hawkish face. "What have you dragged up, Clint?"

"Three settlers from the wagon train. They want to buy some beef, Mr. McGregor."

"None of them looks like settlers. They're Indians," McGregor said. "One's full-blooded, and the other two are half breeds."

Trent nodded. "Good eye. Most men don't see it in me."

"I've killed enough Indians that I know what they look like."

Trent shrugged. "I've killed my share of Indians and palefaces too."

"Yeah, I bet you have. What's with the big dog that followed you here?" McGregor asked, nodding over to where Lobo lay waiting for Trent.

"He's a friend," Trent said. "He's killed men too."

"So you want to buy some steers?"

"Yeah, whatever fifty dollars will buy. The settlers need some fresh meat," Pat said.

"I'm not impressed with your fifty dollars from some future lowdown sodbusters. I hate sodbusters about as much as I hate Indians. They string up fences across my grazing land."

"Well, Mr. McGregor, I guess if you ain't obliged to sell us any beef, we'll mosey back to the wagons," Trent said.

"Do you know you cost me almost a half a day waiting for your wagons to move out so we could cross the trail?" McGregor asked. "Time is money. Each day longer it takes to reach Cheyenne, my cows lose weight, and I lose money. Your wagons cost me money today. I figure you cost me more than fifty dollars today. But I'll take it in payment."

Trent touched his hand to his hat. "Thanks for your time, Mr. McGregor. If I don't get any beef, I reckon I'll hang on to the money." He started to turn Tex around.

A younger version of McGregor stepped in front of Tex. The young cowboy grabbed Tex's bridle. "Indians killed my mother and younger brother."

Lobo picked his ears up and growled, but remained sitting.

"My condolences. Indians killed my mother and father too," Trent said.

The young man suddenly seemed at a loss of words.

Trent shifted his Sharps as he glanced over at McGregor. "If he's your son, you best tell him to let go of my horse."

Pat and Pony Boy tensed up, ready for gunplay.

McGregor glanced at Pat's two Colt Navies. "Gary, back off. We'll deal with them later."

The young man's hand dropped away from Tex's bridle.

McGregor nodded at Trent's rifle. "You any good with that buffalo rifle?"

"He almost killed an entire outlaw gang that planned to attack the wagons," Pat said. "If he can see it, he can kill it."

Trent smiled. "Does that answer your question, Mr. McGregor?"

"You have the eyes of a killer wolf, same as your dog, son," McGregor told Trent.

Trent nodded. "Yup, we do have a few things in common." Without another word, he urged Tex into a trot. Pat and Pony Boy followed him.

"McGregor seems to think a lot of himself. He's an ornery man if I've ever seen one," Pat said as they made a big circle around the herd. "And he said he would take care of us later. What did that mean?"

Trent shook his head. "Probably just jawing. Losing family members will make a man bitter."

"Well, Bruce is going to be disappointed he wouldn't sell any beef," Pat said as they approached the wagons.

"I'll ride out tomorrow and shoot some antelope," Trent said. "I might even bag a mule deer."

"That'll please Bruce."

Maybe Gary will like Becky & save Trent! probably not—

# Chapter Thirteen
# The Stampede

"Where's the cattle?" Bruce asked as the trio rode up to his wagon.

Pat shook his head. "The owner wouldn't sell to us. He said we cost him money today by making him stop the herd. And he hates Indians. He even recognized that Trent had some in him," Pat said, suddenly in a talkative mood.

Bruce glanced at Trent as he dismounted. "He had a sharp eye."

Trent nodded. "He wanted the fifty dollars in payment for having to halt the herd. I thought for a moment we would have to fight our way out of their camp."

Bruce shook his head. "Well, that wasn't very hospitable of him."

"His wife and younger son were killed. He's bitter," Trent said. "And don't worry about fresh meat. I'll spend the day tomorrow hunting."

"Come and get it while it's hot," Lois called out. She and Becky stood beside the cookfire, ready to dish out biscuits and straw-hat gravy.

WAGON MOUND:DO OR DIE | 113

Becky held the plates with biscuits for her mother to ladle gravy over and then handed them out. Trent smiled at Becky when he stepped up to receive his plate.

She smiled back. "I heard you say you would go hunting tomorrow," Becky said.

"Yup, shoot a couple of antelope or maybe a mule deer."

"Good, we can make some stew."

Trent nodded and walked back to sit between Wes and Pat. Lobo whined. When Trent glanced over at him, the big wolf-dog wagged his tail. "I'll save you some," Trent said as he picked up a biscuit and sopped it through the thick gravy. He took a big bite. While he chewed, he glanced over at Pony Boy. "How do you like the white man's food?"

Pony Boy rubbed his belly. "Make Pony Boy fat!"

Wes laughed.

"Frybread will make you fat too," Pat called out as he took a seat nearby.

Lobo growled.

Trent glanced over at the wolf-dog. "What's the matter?"

Lobo jumped to his feet and turned to face the east and howled.

"What's wrong with him?" Bruce asked.

"I'm not sure," Trent said.

Pat placed the palm of his hand against the ground. "Trent!" he shouted. "The ground is shaking."

Trent jumped to his feet. "Stampede!" he shouted as loud as he could. Trent turned to Bruce. "Get everyone into the wagons," he shouted as he bolted for his horse. "Pat, Wes, Pony Boy! Mount up."

The four scrambled for their horses.

the wagons *flew over*
get knocked over

Trent reached Tex first. "Wes, ride around and tell everyone to get in their wagons!"

"Is the stampede heading this way?" Wes asked.

"It sounds like it! Now get!" Trent ordered. "Pat, Pony Boy, if the herd is heading this way, we need to turn them! Shoot the lead cows!" Trent shouted as he spurred toward the rumbling sound. *Fresh meat—on the hoof*

In the fading light, Trent spotted a black mass moving toward the wagons. He galloped Tex straight toward the herd. "Dang it!" he swore as he approached the herd of bellowing, panicked cows. "McGregor is driving the herd toward the wagons. It's not a stampede!" Trent found it hard to believe McGregor would do something so deadly. "He must be crazy," Trent mumbled as he guided Tex to intersect the thundering.

As he rode closer, he could see mounted men waving blankets to drive the cattle. Trent raced across the front of the stampeding herd, lifted his rifle to his shoulder, and shot the leading cow. As he reloaded, Pat and Pony Boy, who had kept pace with Tex, took their clue and started shooting cows as they rode across the front of the herd.

The sound caused the cows to turn south. The men driving the cows started shooting in Trent's direction. Trent aimed at the nearest rider and fired. The man was knocked off his horse. Trent reloaded as he rode in front of the turning herd. He aimed at the next visible rider and quickly knocked him off his horse, too. The other riders took notice of Trent's deadly fire and pulled up.

Yelling and firing their pistols, Pat and Pony Boy turned the herd farther south. Once it was clear, the herd would miss the wagons, Trent signaled Pat and Pony Boy to follow him. He led them out of the path of the stampede and stopped. The three watched the herd slowly pass and vanish into a huge cloud of dust.

"McGregor meant to destroy the wagons," Pat said in his usual calm voice.

"Yup, and he didn't care how many cows he lost," Trent replied.

"He no like us," Pony Boy said.

"Hate is the word," Trent said.

"What do we do now? We can't let this stand," Pat said.

"If we kill McGregor, the law will hunt us down. He's an important man. We can say killing the drovers was an accident, but if I shoot McGregor with the Sharps after the stampede is over, it's murder. These men aren't a bunch of outlaws. They're respected. We kill them, and our names are going to be on a wanted poster," Trent said. "Come on, let's get back and tell Bruce what happened.

"That was close," Bruce said when the three walked up to the wagon. "We could see the cows, they passed so close to the wagons. You turned them just enough to miss us."

"What started the stampede?" Becky asked Trent from the seat of the wagon.

Trent looked at Bruce when he answered. "McGregor drove the cattle at the wagons. It wasn't a stampede."

"What?" Bruce exclaimed. "Why in blazes would they drive the herd toward the wagons?"

"They don't like us," Pony Boy answered.

Bruce looked from Pony Boy to Trent. "Enough to drive the herd into the wagons?"

"He also doesn't like sodbusters. We had to shoot a couple of his cowpokes. So if there wasn't bad blood between us, there is now." Trent paused. "I'm going to swear shooting the riders was accidental, or else we'll be in trouble with the law."

"McGregor wanted to kill all of us?" Becky asked.

"Yup," Trent agreed.

"What about the herd?" Bruce asked.

"They'll stop once McGregor's men stop driving them. I doubt they lost more than fifteen head."

"All I can say is that he must be a bitter man," Bruce said. "Why does he hate settlers?"

"Sodbusters string up fences. They settle on government land, which he uses to graze his cattle. He sees settlers moving west as a threat," Trent explained.

"Hopefully, we've seen the last of Mr. McGregor," Bruce said.

"Don't count on it. He might come around wanting revenge for his dead drovers," Pat said.

Wes patted the handle of his Colt. "Let him come. I'm ready for him."

"Wes!" Bruce called out sharply. "There will be no gunplay! I don't want your name on a wanted poster for killing a rich cattle baron." *he's still only 15*

"Yes, Pa," Wes said, chagrinned. *Just a boy*

"Wes," Trent said. "Let's make the rounds checking the wagons."

"Okay," Wes said, eager to get out of view of his father.

Once the two walked a couple of wagons away, Wes shook his head. "Trent, the man tried to kill us. If you hadn't turned the herd, the cattle would have destroyed the wagons. And there's no telling how many of the settlers would have died."

"That's right, Wes. But if you don't want to go on the dodge from the law, you have to let it slide," Trent said.

"Dadburn it! I hate it," Wes swore.

"So do I, Wes. So do I."

Lobo suddenly growled.

"Riders!" Trent shouted as he ran to the nearest wagon and looked out into the darkness. The moon hadn't risen. It was pitch black beyond the cook fires of the wagons.

A volley of pistol shots rang out as riders galloped around, firing into the circled wagons. Trent shifted his Sharps to his shoulder and listened to the sound of a horse as it passed the wagon. He fired. Someone called out in pain.

"I think you hit someone," Wes said as he fired his pistol into the darkness.

The sound of horses vanished.

Trent ran back to the Cowans' wagon. "Anyone hit?" he shouted.

Bruce, who had pulled Lois and Becky to the ground, was helping them up. "We're okay. Go around and check the wagons," Bruce called out.

"Trent," Pat said as he and Pony Boy ran up. "I got some terrible news. You know Walter, the boy you saved from drowning?"

Trent took a deep breath. "Is he dead?"

"Yup, caught a bullet," Pat said.

"I'll go and talk to his folks. Wes, tell your father not to tell Becky. We'll tell her later. I don't want her to get all upset again." *Still spoiling her —*

"Okay, Trent." Wes started to walk away but paused. "Now can we go and put some of McGregor's men in the dirt?"

Trent shook his head. "No, we would never be able to prove it was his men who attacked us. It was too dark to identify the riders."

Wes sighed and walked away.

"I could take Pony Boy and slip into their camp and kill a few," Pat said.

"No, then it would turn into open war. There are too many of them. A lot of settlers would die. We have to let it go, Pat. They could stampede the herd again in the direction of the wagons. And this time, we might not be so lucky,"

"Sure," his brother said.

Later, when Trent returned from consoling Walter's parents, he found Bruce sitting by the dying cookfire.

Bruce stopped stirring the embers with his stick and glanced up. "Wes told me about the boy."

"The boy's folks are all torn up," Trent said as he squatted across from Bruce.

Bruce took a deep breath. "I don't understand how a man can be so filled with hate that he would attempt to wipe out an entire wagon train. If those cattle had run through the wagons, they would have wrecked them and trampled who knows how many settlers."

"He is probably rich enough to be above the law, Bruce. If he gets the cattle to Cheyenne, he'll make over forty dollars a head in profit. That's a lot of Lincolns."

"Wow, it is at that, Trent. Do you think we've seen the last of Mr. McGregor?" *no — he'll charge you for killing his cows*

"I hope so, Bruce, because if I come across him again, I'll be hard pressed to keep from sending him to boot hill."

The next morning, before the wagons started rolling, all the settlers gathered at a freshly dug grave to bury the little boy. His father carried Walter wrapped in a white sheet to the grave.

Trent stood beside Becky and watched as Bill laid the body in the grave. One of the settlers, a lay preacher, read Psalm 23:4 over the boy when his father stepped aside.

Becky suddenly leaned against Trent's chest and sobbed. Trent hesitantly put his arm over her shoulder. He tried not to look pleased at such a sad moment. But if the truth be told, his heart raced at the touch of Becky's head against his chest. It made him lightheaded.

After Bill shoveled dirt into the grave, Becky lifted her face. "Trent, the man responsible for the boy's death should be hanged. But I don't want you to go after him. You can't touch a rich man like him and get away with it."

"I know, Becky. But one of these days, he'll surely get what he deserves," Trent said.

*Some one was shot — I bet McGregor will lose his son too —*

# Chapter Fourteen
# Wagon Mound

Trent finished his bacon and biscuits. He walked over to Becky and handed her his empty tin plate. "Lobo licked it clean."

"I better put a dent in it so I can tell your plate from the other plates. I think you might be the only one who wants to eat after Lobo."

Trent smiled. "We'll arrive in Wagon Mound this afternoon. I guess you and your mother will do a little shopping."

"Yeah, we have to stock up on supplies for the homestead. Pa's got his heart set on finding a section of land along the Canadian River in Texas."

"It's a nice area. Plenty of water for farming or raising cattle," Trent said.

"Pa's made up his mind on sheep."

"Sheep?" Trent said in a surprised tone.

"Yeah, he says they're easier to manage and need less land. You sell the wool instead of butchering them like you do cattle."

"Well, Texas is mostly cattle country. Ranchers don't cotton to sheep. They say the sheep overgraze and kill the grass."

Becky shrugged. "Pa likes sheep. He's going to try to buy a flock from Wagon Mound. I guess missions usually have sheep. And he heard there's a mission near Wagon Mound."

Trent shrugged. "Okay, sheep, it is." *NO — Trent has to know better*

*Just stupid*

"Trent," Wes called out. "Are you going to lollygag around the cookfire all day?"

"I've got to go and help get the wagons rolling. I'll stop by later," Trent said before he turned and walked over to where Wes held Tex for him. Lobo followed Trent, wagging his tail.

"See, even your dog wants to get moving," Wes said. "I'm excited. We'll be in Wagon Mound today. I've got my heart set on visiting a saloon."

"You would be better off taking one of your pa's bottles of whiskey and sharing it with Pat and Pony Boy in an alley, staying out of the saloon. As I recall, every time we've gone into a saloon, we've gotten into trouble."

"Since when did Trent worry about getting into trouble?" Pat said as he and Pony Boy rode up.

"Since Sis stole his heart. And that's what happens when you get branded, friends," Wes said and laughed.

"Don't you boys have work to do?" Trent said in an irritated tone. "I heard the Wilsons have a busted wheel. Get over and give them a hand."

"Enjoy freedom while you still got it, brother," Pat said before the trio rode off.

In the afternoon, Trent spotted the mission outside of Wagon Mound and rode back to the Cowans' wagon. Bruce and Lois were on each side of the oxen team, and Becky sat in the wagon seat.

"We're an hour away from Wagon Mound," Trent said.

*Some one knock their empty heads together — Forget Sheep — has caused awful range wars —*

Bruce pulled off his hat and slapped it against his britches leg. "God, we've made it. I swear I thought many a time that we wouldn't."

"Have you told the settlers you aren't continuing to California?" Trent asked.

"Yeah, I spoke with the men. They're going to elect another wagon master in Wagon Mound," Bruce said.

"Are any of the others going to join us on the way to Texas?" Trent asked.

"Nope, and to tell you the truth, son, I'm glad. I don't want the responsibility of looking out for others. I want to turn my attention to finding a piece of land to homestead. I read in the newspaper back in Independence that I can homestead one hundred sixty acres, and if I use the Timber Culture Act, I can add another one hundred sixty acres just by planting trees on forty. Trent, that's three hundred and twenty acres. Big enough to farm and raise enough sheep to make a good living."

"Uh, Bruce... you do know that Texas ranchers don't like sheep?" *Hate Them*

"As long as I graze them on my land, I don't see why they would care."

"That's it, though, they do." *A Lot —*

"Well, I'll tell them and the world that I'll do with my land what I want to do," Bruce said in a determined tone.

Trent shrugged. "Okay."

"You want to ride in with Pat and scout out a spot for the wagons?"

"Sure, Tex and Lobo need a good run, and Pat is always ready to race his bangtail," Trent said as he urged Tex into a

*Why is Trent not standing up this time over a very important decision — He's always held his own before — terrible — can be deadly issue!*

trot. As usual, he found Pat with Wes and Pony Boy. The three had become inseparable.

"Trent, don't tell me you got another busted wagon wheel for us to fix," Pat said.

"Nope, Bruce wants you and me to ride into Wagon Mound and scout out a place to gather the wagons."

"Can Pony Boy and I go?" Wes asked.

"Nope, you stay with the wagons. Bruce's orders."

"Then you better not go to the saloon without us," Wes said. "I want to introduce Pony Boy to a saloon and calicoes."

"He might be ready for some whiskey, but a calico? I don't think so," Pat said. "He starts jawing with one of them, and none of us will make it out of the saloon alive."

"Good," Trent said. "Keep that thought in mind when you're in the saloon." He nodded at Pat. "Race you to town."

Trent barely got the words out of his mouth before Pat's mustang bolted off like a racehorse.

"That's all right, Tex. We'll run him down before he gets halfway to Wagon Mound," Trent said as he urged his big stallion into a gallop. Lobo let out a yip and ran after Tex.

Trent caught up with Pat, but not until he was almost at Wagon Mound. "You know I could ride on past you and win the race if'n I wanted to," Trent said.

Pat ignored the comment. "Are you thinking of homesteading next to Bruce?"

"I would need a wagon load of supplies. I can't build a cabin with my bare hands, and I wouldn't ask Bruce for help. Maybe later, after we help him with his cabin and settle a claim. I'll get a job and save up enough money to build my own place and stake out a claim to a hundred sixty acres."

"But I can tell you're hankering to settle down," Pat said.

"It takes two, Pat. And Becky and I are friends, but I don't know how far our friendship goes. She's never given me any hope she wants anything but to be friends."

Pat didn't reply as they approached the town.

Wagon Mound turned out to be a proper town, similar to Council Grove, only smaller. It had a hotel with a restaurant and a saloon. Bars on the window signaled the sheriff's office. And another large building with barred windows was the bank. Scattered along the main street, Trent spotted a dry goods store, a clothing store, a general store, and a livery stable.

"Where will Bruce gather the wagons?" Pat asked.

Trent reined Tex toward the sheriff's office. "Let's go and ask."

"I'll wait outside. I don't like jailhouses," Pat said as Trent dismounted. "Just don't shoot the sheriff."

"Hmm, brother, I do think you just made a joke."

Pat's facial expression didn't alter.

"Lobo, you stay," Trent ordered as he stepped onto the porch. The planks squeaked as Trent approached the door. "Ain't no one going to sneak up on the sheriff," Trent mumbled as he opened the door.

A middle-aged, slightly overweight man sat behind the desk, with his feet propped up and his felt hat pulled down over his face. "Howdy," the man said without moving.

"Thought for sure you were asleep, Sheriff," Trent said as he spotted the badge pinned on the man's brown shirt.

"I'm a light sleeper. The porch is my alarm," the man said as he tilted his hat back, revealing the clean-shaven face of a pleasant-looking man.

"Yup, it is loud."

"What can I do you for?"

"I'm with a large wagon train. We need a place to park the wagons," Trent said.

"West of town, past the cemetery. There's a well and water troughs. How many wagons?"

"Around fifty," Trent said.

"Any trouble on the trail?"

Trent shrugged. "None that we couldn't handle."

"Yup, you look like a capable man. Are you all going on west?"

"The wagon master has plans to sell the trade goods he brought and buy supplies to build a log cabin down Texas way. Along the Canadian River."

"I hear there's some good land around the Canadian. But there are also a bunch of Apaches on the warpath. He'll likely lose his scalp."

"My brother and I'll be going along. We've fought Apaches before. They don't scare us none, Sheriff."

"Yeah, I can see you still have your scalp. I reckon a lot of your success has to do with that Sharps you cradle in the crook of your arm."

"It don't hinder me none," Trent replied.

"Yeah, I bet it don't," the sheriff said.

"I best get back and tell my boss where to take the wagons."

"I hope you boys don't stir up any trouble. I try to maintain a quiet town."

"We certainly ain't looking for no trouble, Sheriff. Some of us might hit the saloon for some whiskey. It's been a while since we could relax with a bottle."

"Just keep your boys under control is all I ask."

"I'll work on that, Sheriff," Trent said as he turned to leave.

"Work hard on it!" the sheriff called after him.

"Well?" Pat asked.

"Ah, he seemed decent."

"Yeah, they always do at first. The hammer usually drops later." Pat handed Trent Tex's reins. "Where to now?"

"Let's mosey over and take a look at the wagon yard. He said it's down the street past the cemetery," Trent said as he turned Tex down the street.

"There's a lot of cowpunchers in town. Maybe McGregor's herd isn't the only one heading north," Pat said.

"Nah, it's more likely ranch hands. The grazing looked good coming into town. I figure there are several large spreads in the area."

Pat shrugged. "I didn't figure Wagon Mound to be such a cow town. I thought it would be more like Council Grove."

"Well, we are farther west," Trent said.

The cemetery seemed large for a town the size of Wagon Mound. He and Pat had battled grave odds since they joined the wagon train.

"Why are you looking at the cemetery?" Pat asked.

"I think we're lucky not to occupy a pine box by now," Trent answered.

Pat shook his head. "Nope. We make our luck. Always have, always will. When you start relying on luck, you might as well crawl into a pine box."

They passed the cemetery and found the wagon yard empty. Trent spotted the well and the watering troughs like the sheriff had said. "It's a good place to rest up before we head back to the Canadian River and down into Texas," Trent said.

"Yeah, my butt could take a few days out of the saddle," Pat said. "Heck, if I get any more bowlegged, I won't need a saddle."

Trent chuckled. "Okay, we've scouted out everything, let's head back to the wagons," he said as he turned Tex around. "Come on, Lobo, let's head home."

# Chapter Fifteen
# The Mission

Bruce took his last bite of bacon as he glanced across the wagon yard. "Dang, if it isn't a relief not to be responsible for fifty wagons. It's as though a heavy burden has been lifted off my shoulders."

Trent nodded in agreement. "Yup, I wish Ralf luck getting them to California." He fed Lobo his last biscuit.

"Trent, don't you be feeding my biscuits to Lobo!" Becky called out from where she helped her mother clean the pots and pans used to cook scrambled eggs, bacon, and biscuits.

"You don't want him to starve, do you?" Trent called back.

"Hmm, I would like to see the day that dog starves! He catches more rabbits than a fox."

Bruce nodded over at the trio. "Where are they heading so early?"

"Pat said he wanted to spend some of his bounty money," Trent replied.

Bruce frowned as he watched his son ride off with Pat and Pony Boy. "Let's ride over to the mission and see if I can buy some sheep. If so, we can gather the sheep on our way to the river. I already got my horse saddled," he said as he headed to the back of the wagon.

Trent tipped his hat. "See you later, Becky."

Becky flashed a smile but didn't reply as Trent mounted Tex. "Come on, Lobo. You ain't going to get any more biscuits."

"Have you thought about claiming a homestead near mine? That is, assuming I find a suitable piece of land down in Texas."

"Yup, I thought hard on it. But I'll wait until we build your log cabin. Then if things look good, I'll homestead a piece near you."

"By looking good, you mean Becky?"

Trent ignored the comment. "Are you sure about sheep instead of cattle?"

"I'm sure. Cattle take too much land and men to handle. I can manage a flock of sheep myself with a dog." Bruce glanced down at Lobo. "But one that won't eat the sheep."

"Yup, there's that," Trent said as they neared a large adobe building with a tall bell tower, curved gables, and wide, projecting eaves. Trent pointed to a grassy meadow near the mission. "They have a large flock of sheep."

A man with a staff stood in the shade of a pine tree as he watched over the flock. Two shaggy dogs moved around the herd, nipping at the heels of the sheep.

"See, I need a dog like that to help," Bruce said.

Trent looked down at Lobo. The sheep and dog had the wolf-dog's full attention. "You think you can do that?"

Lobo glanced up at Trent and whined.

"No, I don't mean kill them all," Trent said and laughed.

A Franciscan monk walked out of the mission to greet them as Bruce dismounted. Trent hung back and held the reins of the horses while Bruce approached the monk. He watched as Bruce made the sign of the cross. Then he watched the two men disappear into the mission. Less than an hour later, Bruce emerged alone.

"Did the holy man sell you some sheep?" Trent asked as Bruce mounted.

*oh too BAD —*

"Yep, half of his flock. But he wouldn't part with either of the dogs. We'll gather the sheep on our way to the Canadian River." *Sheep = trouble — lots of it*

"Maybe you can pick up a puppy in town and train him?" Trent said as they headed back to town.

"Yeah, it's worth a try. But it's going to be rough on me until I get the pup trained."

They didn't speak as they rode through town.

"Put a cowbell on one of the ewes. That way, they'll be easy to locate," Trent said as they approached the cemetery.

"I reckon that'll help," Bruce said as they entered the wagon yard. "Look, someone else brought their wagon in."

"Yup, and it's horse drawn. I think four mares," Trent said. "But wait, that's Pony Boy behind the wagon, and he's leading Leo and Major.

"Well, dang if it ain't," Bruce said as they rode up alongside the wagon.

"Howdy, Pa," Wes called out from the seat of the wagon. Beside him sat Pat, holding the reins to the team of four mares.

"What's going on?" Bruce asked.

Wes smiled. "Pat bought a wagon and supplies for Trent to use when he finds a homestead."

"Pat!" Trent called out.

"I used the bounty money," Pat acknowledged. "I bought two teams of mares so you can start raising horses with Tex as the stud on your homestead. The wagon is full of everything you'll need to build a log cabin: saws, axes, hammers, hinges, and nails. I even bought some panes for the windows."

Trent shook his head. "Well, I guess I have to homestead now." He nodded at Pat and smiled. "Thanks."

Bruce called his wife's name. When she didn't answer, he glanced over at Pat. "Do you know where Lois and Becky are?"

"I saw them at the general store when we drove the wagon through town," Wes answered before Pat had a chance.

"Bruce," Trent said. "I'll go and check on them. Their horses are missing, so they must have ridden to town."

"Good, thanks, Trent. I need to water the oxen. I'll ride to town later to buy the supplies I'll need for the homestead."

Trent nodded before he reined Tex around and headed back to town. He saw Becky and Lois as they walked out of the general store carrying packages. He also spotted three cowhands lounging around on the porch of the general store in straight chairs. One rose out of his chair at the sight of the two women and walked toward them. As Trent dismounted, he heard the man addressing Becky.

"Hey there, lassie, you look like you could use some help. Let me carry that for you," the big, bearded man in a brown battered felt hat and dirty dungarees said when he stepped in front of Becky.

"Thank you kindly, sir, but we can manage," Lois called out.

"I'm not asking to help you. You are too long in the teeth for my taste. I'm asking the young, pretty one."

"Be so kind as to step aside and let us by, mister," Becky demanded.

"Oh, yeah, I like a young filly with spirit," the cowhand said.

"Mister," Trent said as he approached the porch. "Do yourself a favor and sit back down."

The man turned to face Trent. He looked to be in his thirties, with a lined face and cruel eyes. "I don't reckon I'm talking to you, boy. You best get back on your pony and head for the mountains or else daddy may spank you."

Trent stepped onto the porch, and the other two men stood and faced him. "I don't want trouble, mister," Trent said as he shifted his Sharps in the crook of his arm. "Now step aside before I blow a fist-sized hole in that big gut of yours."

"Trent," Becky called his name.

"Okay, I'll just blow his hand off."

A look of concern clouded the man's face.

"He's drunk, Trent. Don't hurt him," Becky said as she walked around the man.

The man reached for Becky's arm. Before he touched her, Trent stepped forward and brought the stock of his Sharps up to hit the man under the chin. The big man fell backward and hit the planks with a loud thud. The other two men started to reach for their irons, only to find themselves staring down the barrel of the buffalo rifle.

Trent motioned with the barrel of the rifle. "Lift him to his feet and head home, boys."

The men hesitated a moment before hurrying forward and grabbing the big man to pull him to his feet. "Wake up, Riley," one of the men called out as he slapped the man's face.

"Let me take your packages," Trent said as he approached Becky and Lois. "I'll strap them onto my saddle if there is nothing breakable." *now his hands are full*

"Just clothes," Becky said as she and her mom handed Trent the packages.

"Towns like Wagon Mound aren't safe for women alone," Trent said.

"Oh, I can take care of myself," Becky surprised Trent by saying. She reached into her drawstring purse and pulled out a derringer. "I bought it inside. The next man who confronts me, I'll give him a surprise."

Trent glanced at Lois in shock.

"It was Becky's idea, not mine," her mother said. "The clerk took her behind the store and showed Becky how to load and shoot it."

"Trent, I decided if I'm going to live on the frontier, then I've got to adjust."

Trent nodded. "Getting a derringer is a big adjustment." After he tied the packages on his saddle, Trent helped first Lois and then Becky onto their horses.

"Did you already see the wagon and supplies that Pat bought for your homestead?" Lois asked.

"Yup, the skunk went completely behind my back," Trent called out as he mounted.

"He said it was the only way," ~~Becky said~~. "So I guess it's now official. You'll be staking a claim for a homestead."

"I reckon so," Trent said as he rode beside Becky. "Of course, we have to find some land suitable for homesteading first.

"I hear Texas is a big place. I'm sure there's a spot for Pa and you to homestead," Becky said and smiled.

"Did Bruce get his sheep?" Lois asked.

"Yup, got a sizable flock. Guess you'll have wool to weave sweaters and mutton to eat in the future," Trent said. *Yuck*

"You don't sound enthusiastic," Lois said.

"Well, Texas is cattle country. The big ranchers don't cotton to sheepherders."

"I don't see a problem if we keep the sheep on our homestead," Lois said. *that is the problem*

"That's the thing about cattle and sheep, they like to wander where they shouldn't," Trent said. "But it'll be okay. *Won't* I'll watch over them." He glanced down at Lobo. "And so will Lobo."

"Yeah," Lois said. "I reckon he'll watch over what he doesn't eat."

# Chapter Sixteen
# The Canadian River

Trent reined Tex to a stop as he looked back at the two wagons. Bruce's oxen-drawn wagon set the pace, with his horse-drawn wagon pulling up the rear. Pat drove his wagon. Wes and Pony Boy herded the flock of thirty sheep with the help of Lobo, who had surprised everyone and taken to herding with a passion. After him ran a shaggy yelping female puppy.

Trent turned back and continued riding. He wanted to scout out the river. The wagons wouldn't cross, but still, Trent wanted to have a look-see. The plan he and Bruce had settled on dictated that they follow the Canadian River down into Texas. And after they crossed into Texas, they'd start looking for a suitable homestead alongside the river.

Since he was about two miles from the river, he let Tex stretch his legs at a full gallop. The long-legged stallion ate up the ground in a hurry. When Trent spotted the ponderosa pines growing along the riverbank, he slowed Tex to a walk to cool him down.

The sight that confronted Trent caused him to shift the rifle in the crook of his arm and stop Tex. Along the near bank of the river, stood at least fifty mounted Indians. He couldn't tell their tribe from so far away. However, he found himself hoping they weren't Arapahos.

With a sigh, Trent urged Tex forward. As he approached the river, his worst fear materialized. Chief Two Moons sat astride his pony at the head of the column of warriors. Trent immediately knew the reason the chief had tracked the wagon train to Wagon Mound. Revenge for the killing of his son, One Moon. Trent didn't have to be told that Two Moons wanted Pony Boy's scalp.

Trent knew he probably could kill the chief with his Sharps, but figured that wouldn't end the feud. The chief's men would attack the wagons the moment he killed their chief. Nope, this had to be settled, one way or another.

Although Trent didn't know sign language as well as Pat, he figured he knew enough to see what Chief Two Moons had in mind. With that thought in mind, he rode closer and stopped to see if the Chief meant to parley.

After a long moment, Chief Two Moons shouted something to his men and then rode out to meet Trent. They exchanged signs of greetings. But that was the last of the friendly signs. After that, it was demands that Trent turn over Pony Boy to Chief Two Moons or face his anger.

Trent refused. He struggled with the signs but finally told the chief it would dishonor him to give Pony Boy to Two Moons, that Pony Boy had become his brother. He would fight the chief before he would surrender his brother.

Chief Two Moons made the sign that he would attack.

Suddenly, Trent got an idea. A dangerous one, but better than fighting a war party of heavily armed men. He had to think hard to remember the signs he needed to make.

Finally, Trent moved his hands with confidence as he challenged Chief Two Moons to a duel to the death. If the chief lived, he could have Pony Boy, but if Trent survived, then Two Moons's warriors would take the chief's body and return to their tribe.

A smile played across the Arapaho chief's face. He nodded in agreement. He made the sign for the fight to start now. Trent shook his head. He pointed back the way he had come and signaled that he must fetch Pony Boy first. After mulling it over, Two Moons agreed.

Satisfied, Trent turned Tex around and rode toward the wagons at a fast gallop. Everyone seemed to be watching Trent as he approached. Bruce looked concerned when Trent stopped Tex beside him.

"What now? Don't tell me we're in for some more bad luck," Bruce declared.

"I'm afraid so. Chief Two Moons tracked us to Wagon Mound," Trent explained.

"What does he want?" Bruce asked.

"He wants us to hand over Pony Boy," Trent said. "But I refused."

"Are we all going to die over the boy?" Bruce asked.

Trent shook his head. "No, I'm going to have a duel with the chief. If he wins, he gets Pony Boy. If I win, his men return home."

Becky, who could hear them from her seat on the wagon, called out, "What kind of duel?"

Trent glanced at Becky and hesitated.

"Trent, what kind of duel?" Becky repeated.

"To the death with knives."

"No! No! Trent, no!"

"It was the only way I could keep Two Moons from attacking. And, Becky, even as good as Pat and I are with pistols and my rifle, we can't stop a charge of so many armed men."

Wes walked up. "Why are we stopped?"

Trent told him the situation and asked him to go tend the sheep and send Pony Boy to him. A little later, the young man, who no longer looked entirely Arapaho, ran up to Trent.

"Get your horse. Chief Two Moons is waiting at the river. He wants revenge for your having killed his son, One Moon.

"I will go to him to prevent bloodshed," Pony Boy said immediately.

Trent shook his head. "No, I challenged Two Moons to a duel to the death. If I lose, then you will have to go with him back to the tribe. But I don't intend to lose! Now, get your horse."

Pat walked up from his wagon. "What's happening? Why are we stopped?"

Trent sighed and explained the situation to his brother. "Pat, you are not going with us, and that's final. I need you and Wes here to protect Becky, as things can go wrong even if I win. The young bucks are unpredictable. Maybe they'll honor Two Moons's word and maybe not."

"Okay, okay, but you better not go and get yourself killed and waste the supplies I bought you," Pat declared, with the most emotional facial expression Trent had seen since they were small boys.

Trent smiled. "Don't worry, I'm not ready for boot hill." Then before Becky, Wes, or Bruce could say anything else, he glanced down at Lobo. "You stay," he said before he gave Tex his bit and urged the big stallion into a gallop.

Pony Boy spurred his horse and bolted after Trent.

The entire war party had dismounted. They sat in a large circle on this side of the bank with Chief Two Moons in the middle of the circle. The chief had stripped down to his leggings. His body bulged with muscles as he walked around the circle while he waited for Trent.

Trent dismounted and handed his rifle and gun belt to Pony Boy. "If I win, toss me my pistol and be prepared for us to shoot our way out if attacked."

"They will honor the wishes of Two Moons. To do otherwise would dishonor him," Pony Boy said.

"Yup, but be ready anyway. There are always some men who have less honor than others."

"I will kill any who try to stop you from leaving the circle, should you survive. But know this, Two Moons has had many knife duels."

"Yup, I can see the scars," Trent said a little grimly as he pulled out his bowie knife.

The circle of men parted to allow him to enter and then closed behind Trent. Chief Two Moons spoke.

Trent glanced over at Pony Boy, who stood behind the first row of men. "He will cut your heart out and eat it," Pony Boy translated.

"Fly at it," Trent said.

Pony Boy looked puzzled.

"Tell him I'm ready," Trent rephrased his statement.

Pony Boy nodded and spoke to the chief who also held a knife.

Trent figured Two Moons would charge, and he did. The man rushed forward and slashed with his knife. However, Trent had sidestepped like a boxer and danced out of reach. Two Moons roared in anger and shouted at Trent.

"He says you fight like a woman, you run away," Pony Boy called out.

"Tell him he fights like a clumsy bull," Trent replied.

After Pony Boy relayed Trent's message, the chief growled like a bear and charged again. Trent sidestepped, but Two Moons had anticipated his move and matched his shift in position. He slashed at Trent. The blade of the knife cut through Trent's shirt and the flesh covering his left ribs.

*really* — "Ouch!" Trent said and grinned as he danced out of reach of the follow-up slashing motion of Two Moons's knife. "Hmm, Becky is going to have to sew both me and my shirt up."

Two Moons rushed forward again, intent on finishing Trent off. This time, Trent didn't sidestep. Instead, he dropped under the chief's blade as Two Moons slashed at him. The knife passed harmlessly over Trent's head and left him open for a counterattack. And Trent did just that. He sprung forward as he rose to his feet and lashed out with his knife. The blade raked across Two Moons's belly, cutting deep.

A shout of disbelief erupted from the men as entrails spilled out. Two Moons tried to catch his guts with his hands. However, they slipped off the palm of his hands and dropped to the ground. Two Moons kneeled. From that position, he glanced up at Trent. And then he spoke to his men.

"He is telling them they must honor him by not attacking you or the wagon train. That Pony Boy is free to live with the white man."

A murmur of discontent ran through the circle of warriors. One grabbed his knife and charged Trent. He only made it halfway before a pistol shot rang out. The man grabbed his chest and crumpled to the ground. Trent looked at Pony Boy. Gunsmoke rose from the barrel of his pistol.

Two Moons called out weakly, chastising the warrior for disobeying him before he fell face-first into the dirt. Warriors rushed to Two Moons's side.

"We go now," Pony Boy declared as he offered Trent his rifle and gun belt.

"Yup, I think that's wise," Trent said as he buckled on the gun belt and then grabbed the Sharps. "Let's hightail it back to the wagons before more decide to take matters into their own hands."

As the two rode off, the warriors started a death chant.

"God, when Becky sees all the blood on my shirt, she's going to faint." *let her —*

# Epilogue
# Welcome to Texas

"Stay still, Trent. I can't sew you up if you keep fidgeting around," Becky said.

"Feels like you have a dull needle," Trent complained. "Ouch!"

Becky giggled.

*she is the baby*

"You did that on purpose!"

"Quit being such a baby. It's just a few stitches," Wes said from outside the wagon.

"Another word and I'll have her sew your mouth shut," Trent replied.

"Now, that I would like to have done years ago," Becky said as she broke the thread and tied it in a knot. "I'm finished. Now you can run along and get shot, cut, or clubbed."

"You lack a proper bedside manner," Trent said as he buttoned his shirt.

"You should know. You must have spent a lot of time getting sewed up by doctors from all the scars on your body," Becky said.

"Nah," Pat said as he poked his head into the wagon. "Mama sewed him up. He was always getting in fights with the boys from the different towns we passed through. I think the word is antisocial."

Becky nodded. "Now the truth comes out. I guess that antisocial thing explains why you always carry that rifle in the crook of your arm."

"Hmm, I don't have to get in another fight. I'm getting pretty beat up right now," Trent said as he climbed out of the wagon.

Trent walked behind the wagon where he had tied Tex.

"I guess needle and thread wouldn't have saved Two Moons," Pat said.

"Nope, I must have cut something that made him bleed like a stuck pig," Trent said.

"From what Pony Boy told me, it could have been you bleeding out on the ground instead of Two Moons."

"Well, it wasn't," Trent said in a dismissive tone. "Now let's get the wagons moving. I don't want to stop near the crossing. I want to make tracks down the river a way before we stop for the night."

"Yeah, I want to put as much distance between us and the Arapahos as possible," Pat agreed.

"How is Pony Boy acting since the duel?" Trent asked as he mounted Tex.

"I think you have a lap dog. Pony Boy can't stop talking about how you defeated Two Moons. And to be honest, he loves herding the sheep. I think he's found his calling. Before this, I would have bet the pot that he would have rode with Wes and me later when we head west. However, I don't think he's going to get very far from you and those sheep."

"Maybe. Time will tell," Trent said as he guided Tex back to the front of the wagon.

Bruce and Lois stood on opposite sides of the oxen.

"Let's get them moving, Bruce," Trent called out. "We're burning daylight."

"Trent," Becky said. "You get back and drive your team. You don't need to be riding for a few days."

"Yes, doc," Trent called over his shoulder.

Wes caught up with Trent. "Roped and branded for sure," he said and laughed.

"Stop," Trent said. "Don't make me laugh. It hurts."

"She took your horse, and next it will be your rifle," Wes added.

Trent shook his head. "I ain't giving up my rifle."

"You say that now. I'll remind you when I see you without the Sharps in your arm." *We'll see —*

"Ain't going to happen," Trent said as he dismounted and tied Tex to the back of his wagon. He walked to the front and climbed into the seat. "You get back there and help Pony Boy with the sheep."

"He don't need help. He's got Lobo and Pup. Never thought I would see Lobo herding sheep—killing them, yeah, herding them no."

As Pat rode up, Trent said, "Pat, ride ahead and scout downriver for a place to camp tonight. And make sure all the Arapaho are gone. Here, you better take the Sharps in case there's trouble."

"I don't expect any more trouble from them, but there are plenty of Apaches in the area. I wouldn't doubt it if they're spying on us." *Of course they are — alot of them*

"Let's hope not. I've had enough fighting for one day," Trent called out as Pat rode ahead.

They reached the water's edge an hour later and turned downriver, following the bank through the flat grassy prairie. In the distance, they could see a line of tall canyons that would take days to reach.

Trent had to admit that Becky had been right. He was in no shape to be riding a horse. The wound ached like bees were stinging him constantly as each breath put pressure on the stitches.

Trent didn't see Pat ride up since he was behind the Cowans' wagon. He only knew his brother had returned when he heard his voice. As much as he would have liked to have run up and jawed with Pat and Bruce, he waited patiently for Pat to come to him.

"What did you find downriver?" Trent asked when his brother finally came back to him.

"No signs of hostiles. If there are Apaches around, they're keeping out of sight like only they can do," Pat said. "I found a good spot among a group of ponderosas to stop for the night. If there are pines like these down in Texas, we're going to have plenty of logs for the cabins. But, dang, it's going to be hard work cutting and hauling."

"It's a good thing Bruce has two teams of oxen," Trent said.

"Yup, they're going to come in right handy. Well, I'll go back and jaw a bit with Wes and Pony Boy. See you later," Pat called out as he rode off to the rear.

By the time they reached the site Pat had picked out for the night, Trent felt lightheaded. He stumbled as he climbed off the wagon. Pat noticed and jumped off his horse just in time to catch his brother as he collapsed.

\*\*\*

Bruce stopped the oxen and surveyed the broad river valley that lay before them. He smiled when Trent walked up to stand beside him. "The dead has arisen. For a time, I thought we had lost you. But Becky said your fever broke last night.

"Yup, I'm still a little shaky on my feet. But I'm getting better by the minute."

Bruce stretched his hands out. "So this is Texas."

"Yup, actually, we've been moving through Texas for a couple of days, according to Pat."

"Do you know the name of the valley yonder?"

"Nope, I doubt it's been settled since canyons and dry washes surround the valley. Settlers don't usually follow the Canadian River down into Texas like we did. Pat said there were some steep spots, that it took both the team of horses and oxen to pull the wagons over the ridges."

"Yeah, and they were narrow to boot—barely room for the wagons. We're lucky we made it over the passes," Bruce said.

"There's good grazing down in the valley. And lots of trees along the river," Trent said. "I think we've found a spot to homestead."

"How far do you think the nearest town is?" Bruce asked.

"Well, since we're in the canyons, I think Salt Flats lies north once you get past them. I would say three days by oxen-drawn wagon, much less by horseback. Now the next major town would be Dumas, further north and east of here."

"You seem to know Texas well," Bruce said.

"Like I said before, we traveled with Daddy trading all through Texas."

"I think we'll camp here for the night and move down into the valley tomorrow," Bruce said. "I can't wait to start looking for a place to homestead. I don't see any ranches. I guess the entire valley is unsettled."

"Even if there's a sodbuster or two, there's plenty of room left," Trent said. "I better get back and say hello to Tex."

"Lobo has been visiting the wagon regularly to check on you," Bruce said. "He worries over you almost as much as Becky."

Trent smiled from ear to ear before he walked away. Pat and Wes found Trent stroking Tex on the shoulder.

"He visits his horse before he does us, Pat," Wes called out. "I guess we know how we rank."

"A mite above a skunk," Trent said as he smiled at Wes. He glanced around. "Where is Pony Boy?"

"He's with his sheep. They ain't Bruce's anymore, he's claimed them. Heck, he sleeps out with the flock, him, Lobo, and Pup," Wes said and chuckled.

"When do we start cutting down trees for the log cabins?" Pat asked.

"Soon, I don't think it's going to be hard for Bruce and me to find land to homestead."

"Pat and I will stick around until the cabins are built and you and Pa get settled. After that, we're heading west."

"No Pony Boy, really?"

Pat shook his head. "He's turned into a shepherd. He ain't leaving his flock."

"I better get back to the wagon before Becky comes looking for me with a frying pan in her hand."

"Wow, he's doubled branded now," Wes called out as Trent walked away.

### The End

Thanks for taking the time to read this story. A positive review on Amazon would be appreciated.

*[handwritten note: Bottom — See he's already henpecked + under her thumb — Finally — book 3 + I'll be done! Then I can read a real book again!]*

Made in the USA
Coppell, TX
25 July 2020

31753742R00090